This book belongs to - - -

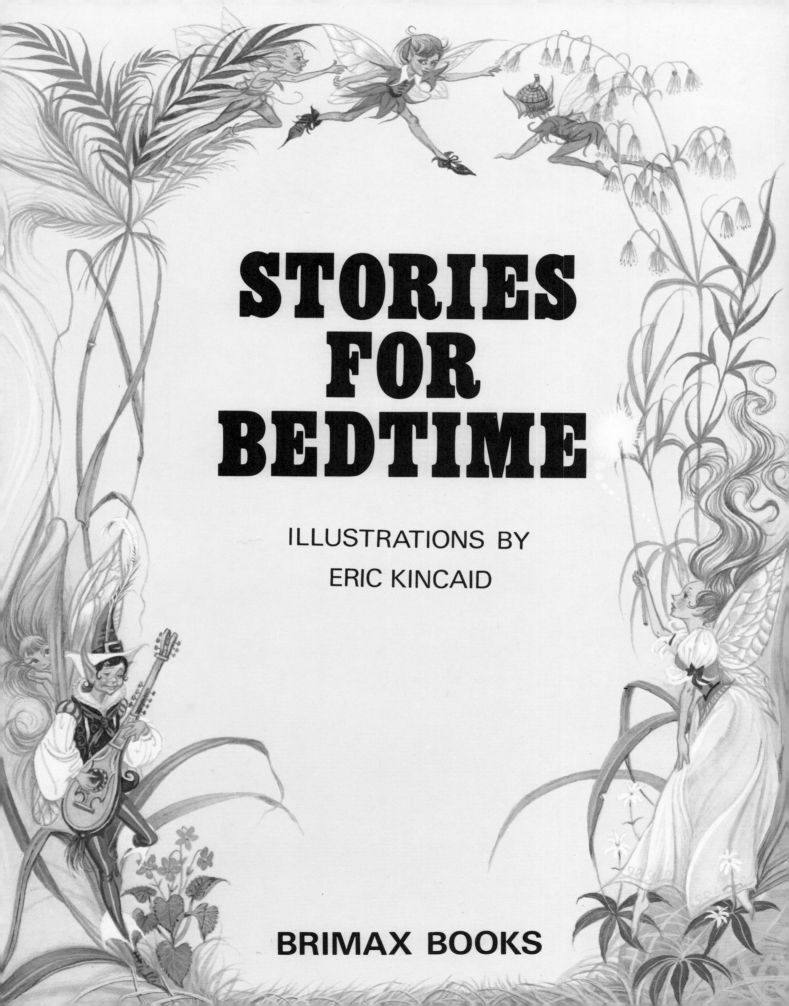

STORIES FOR BEDTIME

ILLUSTRATIONS BY

ERIC KINCAID

BRIMAX BOOKS

ISBN 0 86112 393 X
© BRIMAX BOOKS LTD. All rights reserved
Published by BRIMAX BOOKS, Newmarket, England 1986
This book is a revised edition of 'Bedtime Stories'
Omnibus first published by Brimax Books 1979.
Printed in Hong Kong

NO BUTTER FOR HIS BREAD

It was breakfast time and the Master wanted butter for his bread.

"Molly!" he called to the dairy maid, "Bring me butter for my bread."

"I can't sir," said Molly.

"Can't!" said the Master. "No such word as can't," and then he added, "Why can't you?"

"Because there is no butter," said Molly.

"No butter!" The Master jumped from his chair and knocked it with a clatter to the floor. "No butter. . . .what do you mean NO BUTTER!!!!"

"There is no butter in the dairy. There is no butter in the kitchen," said Molly.

She righted the Master's chair. He sat down again and glared. He didn't frighten Molly. She knew he was gentle as butter himself underneath his crusty outside. And she knew how much he liked butter on his bread.

"Why isn't there any butter?" he stormed.

"Because. . . ." said Molly. "Because. . . ."

"You're the milk maid. . . ." roared the Master, "Go to the dairy and make me some." He was getting hungry and he couldn't eat bread without butter. He knew he was getting bad tempered. He didn't like being bad tempered.

"Sir," said Molly as though he wasn't shouting at all. "I've been in the dairy since six. The cream in the churn will not turn into butter."

"Don't be ridiculous!" shouted the Master. And jumping from his chair, again knocking it to the floor with a clatter, he marched to the dairy with his napkin caught on his waistcoat button, and with Molly running after him not in the least flustered.

The dairy was cool and airy, and it cooled the Master's temper. "I'm sorry I shouted Molly," he said, "But you know how I like my butter. . .and you really mustn't say there isn't any butter when all you have to do is churn it. Now be a good girl and start churning. . ."

"Very well," said Molly. If the Master wouldn't believe her then he would have to see for himself. "Surely it's ready now," said the Master who was pacing backwards and forwards in front of Daisy the cow so quickly that she was beginning to wonder if she should toss him over the moon. "Here. . .let me look." Molly took the lid off the churn. The cream from Daisy's milk was pale as the palest primrose and as fluid as the water in the pond. "What's the matter with it?" demanded the Master.

"What's the matter with your milk?" he demanded of Daisy the cow.

Daisy looked at him with her large brown eyes and mooed. Her moo could have meant anything.

"What's to be done?" demanded the Master.

"Well it seems to me as though it has had a spell put on it," said Molly.

"Spell. . .rubbish!" said the Master.

"Then why won't it turn?" asked Molly.

"Well, what are you waiting for? How do you break a spell?" asked the Master impatiently. He was getting so hungry for bread and butter he was prepared to believe anything and try anything.

"We could try holding it over running water?" said Molly.

That's how it was that the Master's wife found the Master standing in the middle of the stream in the middle of the meadow holding a milk churn over his head.

"Come out of there at once, your feet are getting wet," she scolded.

The Master did as he was told and water and fishes poured from his shoes.

"Drat," he said, as he shook the churn. "It's still sloshing about."

He thought he had better explain to his wife who was dropping the stranded fish back into the stream.

"There's a spell on the milk. It won't churn. I haven't had breakfast. I'm hungry. I want my bread and butter. What shall I do?"

"Tie a rowan sprig to it, dear," said his wife sweetly. "Everyone knows that's how a spell is broken."

There just happened to be a rowan tree close by the dairy. But a sprig tied to the churn made not the slightest difference to the milk.

"So that always works, does it?" said the Master huffily. "What else always works?"

"Horseshoes over the dairy door," said the Master's wife.

There were so many horseshoes over the dairy door there wasn't room for another one.

The Master's wife wanted her husband to buy her a new dress, so she just had to think of something. She thought and thought and could think of nothing. Molly sat beside her and thought and thought and also thought of nothing. The Master churned and churned till his arms ached and his hair was wet with perspiration.

"Who would want to put a spell on a churn of milk?" he panted as he stopped to catch his breath. "It's no one who likes butter that's for sure!"

Molly and the Master's wife looked at one another. Both knew exactly what the other was thinking.

"Molly," said the Master's wife. "Get your bonnet."

"Where are you going?" asked the Master.

"To visit the witch who lives at the mill," said his wife.

"Don't be silly. She likes butter. I've heard she likes butter as much as I do."

"Liking has nothing to do with it," said his wife. "Having, has. . .and I've heard that her butter churn fell over and broke into a hundred pieces."

"Stuff and nonsense," muttered the Master, and went back to his own churning.

Molly and the Master's wife went straight to the mill before their courage failed them. Neither of them would have dared to go alone.

"Yes," said the witch when they questioned her, very politely and very carefully, of course. It doesn't do to upset a witch. "My butter churn IS broken and I can't find the right spell to mend it. I have put a spell on all the unbroken churns. I have no butter so no one else shall."

"Yes," said the witch. "I will take off the spell if you promise to bring me a large pat of freshly made butter every other day."

When Molly and the Master's wife got home, the Master was dancing a jig in the dairy and Daisy was mooing.

"I did it. . .I found the answer. . .it's turned to butter."

"No, you didn't," said the Master's wife. "Now you go straight this minute and take some of that butter to the witch at the mill."

"Why? Why should I?" demanded the Master. But of course, as soon as his wife told him why he should he scooped some into a bowl. He ran all the way to the mill and left it on the witch's doorstep and then he ran all the way home again and had a late breakfast, while his wife went to town and bought a new dress and Molly swept out the dairy and crooned to Daisy the cow.

"He'll be up there for hours,"
he said. "Now is my chance to
steal his book of spells." And
first making sure that there was no
one to observe him he crept along
the lane and up the path towards
the Squire's big house. He pushed
open the door and crept inside.
It was still, and very quiet, with
not even a ticking clock to break
the silence.

He pushed open the study door.
There was a book with its pages
lying open on the desk. Was that
it?

He paused, and waited and
listened. He didn't want to be
caught in the act of taking it.

Up on the hill, something made
the Squire feel prickly behind his
ears and down the back of his spine.
There was something wrong. . .somewhere.

"Whoa!" he cried to his horse. They pulled up sharply at
a point where they could see the rooftops of the village and the
roof of the Squire's own house.

He remembered he had left his book of spells open on his desk.
Suppose. . .just suppose someone got hold of it. Someone who didn't
understand how careful you had to be with magic spells. The
damage might be so awful it could never be repaired. He couldn't
remember locking the front door either. Perhaps there was someone
stealing his book at this very moment.

He had to get home quickly. He whispered to his horse and they took the quickest way down, which happened to be straight over the rooftops. They nearly fell and broke all their bones when the horse's hoof caught one of the pinnacles on the church tower, but by a firm strong pull on the reins on the part of the Squire and a frantic kick by the horse they managed to land bumpily, but safely.

The Squire ran to his house. He was only just in time. Little Billy was just sneaking out of the front door with the spell book under his arm.

"Mine, I believe," said the Squire. And Billy found himself without the spell book and sitting in the fish pond with a waterlily tucked over his ear and a toad croaking at his elbow. . .

"Oh..oh.." he moaned. "He'll turn *me* into a toad. . . I know he will. . ." The Squire didn't say he would and he didn't say he wouldn't. Instead he looked at Billy sternly and said, "Go home, boy." Which Billy did, trailing water weed and waterlilies from his breeches.

As for the Squire, he was so relieved to have saved the village from disaster, that he resolved from that day onwards always to keep his book of spells under lock and key, and that is just what he did.

A PIECE OF ROPE

I've slung a rope up in a tree,
It's hanging from a branch;
But when I mount and swing away
It's my stallion on the ranch.

He's swift and strong, a champion;
My friend, so sure and true;
We'll track down all the 'baddies'
Like cowboys in Westerns do.

We help to drive the cattle,
We cross the scorching plain;
We outshoot any ambush
Set up to kill for gain.

Then when we've made our journey,
And arrive 'all-in' – work done,
I tether up my splendid steed
And put away my gun.

If the 'baddies' ever get me
I'll be very brave – I hope;
But of course it's only a lovely game;
And my horse – just a piece of rope!

20

NED OF THE TODDIN

Once upon a time, there was a little tortoiseshell kitten with pointed ears and a twitchy tail. His name was Ned of the Toddin, which was rather a strange name, but it was the only one he had, and he soon got used to it. His mother's name was Waowhler, and his father's name was Skaratch, and they all lived together on an emerald green bank between an old stone farmhouse and a brambly wood.

Now you could tell that Ned of the Toddin was not an ordinary kitten, because he began to look out for mice when he was only two hours old. When he was only two days old, he could skip about and talk better than most grown-up cats. When he was only three days old he was a full-size furry kitten, and when he was four days old he began to go out on his adventures.

First of all he trotted daintily up to the old stone farmhouse when nobody was about, just to see what it was like. There on the grey stone step were three bottles of snow-white milk with shiny silver tops.

"Give me some milk," cried Ned, "or I'll knock your tops off with my twitchy tail."

But the milk bottles just stood there, as deaf as three white posts, and didn't do anything at all. So Ned went up to the first milk bottle and carefully pressed its silver top with his twitchy tail. Then he took it between his furry paws and drank all the milk out of it. GULP. GULP. GULP. Just like that. Then he went up to the second milk bottle and pressed its silver top carefully with his twitchy tail. Then he took it between his furry paws and drank all the milk out of that too. But when he came to the third, he had really had enough, so he drank no more than the smooth cream off the top. LAP. LAP. LAP. Just like that. It was delicious. When the farmer came to look for his milk he was very surprised indeed to find most of it gone.

"Well I don't know," he said.

In the meantime, Ned of the Toddin went skipping gaily over the emerald green grass towards the sparkling river that ran along behind the farmhouse. Now an ordinary kitten is very frightened indeed of water, but Ned didn't mind it a bit. There he stood, on the riverside, and as he looked down into the sparkling water he could see a lot of little fish swimming lazily about in the sunshine, for all the world as if it was a Sunday, with nothing to do.

"Come up and be eaten, little fish," cried Ned, "or I'll splash all of the water out of the river with my twitchy tail."

But the little fish were far too busy doing nothing to listen to Ned, and they just went on swimming lazily about in the sunshine.

"Come up and be eaten, little fish," cried Ned again, "or I'll knock all your scales off with my twitchy tail."

But the little fish could not hear what Ned was saying. They just went on swimming round and round in the sparkling water. So Ned jumped straight into the river and gobbled up all the lazy fish. GOBBLE. GOBBLE. GOBBLE. Just like that.

Then he sprang merrily out of the water onto the river side. He shook himself so hard that the little water drops made a rainbow in the sunshine.

"That's better," he said.

Then he went on his way for all the world like an ordinary kitten who is simply out for a stroll among the daisies and dandelions.

He hadn't gone very far when he came upon a rather muddy pigsty. Inside the pigsty was a very large pig indeed. He had pink flapping ears, and pink trotters, and a curly pink tail. His name was Groanergut Swilltrough, and he was the most bad-tempered pig in the neighbourhood. As soon as he saw Ned he gave an unfriendly little grunt. GHHHH. Just like that.

"Go away, little kitten," he said. "I haven't got time for you today." Groanergut kicked several pieces of mud at Ned as he stood in the entrance to the pigsty.

"If you do that again," said Ned. "I'll knock your ears flat with my twitchy tail."

Groanergut Swilltrough gave a horrid little squeal. EEEEE. Just like that. Then he kicked some much larger pieces of mud at Ned. Any ordinary kitten would have run away, but Ned was not an ordinary kitten by a long way. All he did was hit Groanergut's piggy nose with his twitchy tail. WOP. Just like that.

"SQUEEEEEAL!" said Groanergut, looking very shocked indeed. He got as much mud as he could, and tried to kick it over Ned, but Ned skipped cleverly out of the way, and it all missed. Then Groanergut ran up to Ned, and tried to squash him into the mud, but Ned pulled his flapping ears over his eyes with his twitchy tail, so that he couldn't see where he was going. He bumped into the side of the pigsty with a terrible THUD. Just like that.

"EEEEEE," said Groanergut. He lay there exhausted.

In the meantime, Ned of the Toddin went happily on his way across the emerald green grass, all sprinkled on with snow-white daisies. He went past the old stone farmhouse, and he was just on his way home when he smelled a delicious smell. He sniffed, and sniffed again, but he didn't know what it was because he was only four days old, and you couldn't expect him to know *everything*. SNIFF. SNIFF. SNIFF. He followed the smell all the way back to the old farmhouse. It led him over the grey stone step, and into the spotless white kitchen.

There, on the wooden table, was a beautiful piece of yellow cheese. Ned sniffed carefully. No doubt about it. The smell led right up to the cheese. Quick as a flash Ned jumped onto the table and ate up the cheese. SWILLOWSWALLOW. Just like that.

"That was delicious," he said.

Just then he heard someone coming, so he jumped straight down off the wooden table and went quietly out through the door. When the farmer's wife saw that her cheese had gone she was very surprised indeed.

"Well I don't know," she said.

As soon as he got home, Ned the Toddin told his mummy and daddy all he had done during the day. Skaratch and Waowhler raised their furry eyebrows, because they had never heard of such an extraordinary kitten before.

"Well," said Skaratch.

"Well," said Waowhler.

So Ned curled up on a patch of soft moss and went to sleep, because he really was a bit tired after his adventures. There he lay, in a little tortoiseshell bundle, for all the world like a quiet well-behaved kitten of whom any mother could be proud.

"PRRRRRR," he said. "PRRRRRR."

BESSIE THE ELEPHANT

Bessie the elephant blushed with shame;
She had forgotten her name, her name.
She asked the stork, but he would not tell,
The parrot he merely said "Well well."
She asked the lion, who roared with laughter,
And ten little monkeys came giggling after.
She asked the hippo, who yawned aloud,
The stately peacock was much too proud.
The donkey he merely gave a bray,
The dormouse was shy, and couldn't say.
Bess blew her trumpet: "Oh tell me do."
Then all of them answered: "You are you!"

27

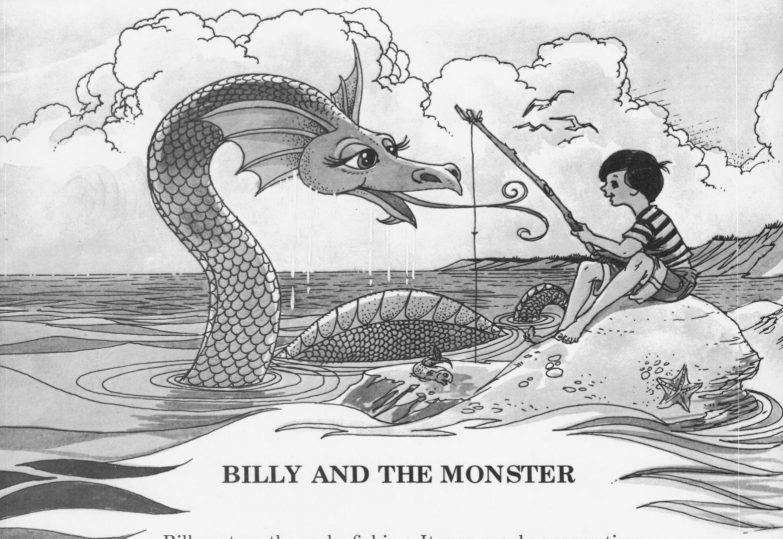

BILLY AND THE MONSTER

Billy sat on the rocks fishing. It was nearly supper time and he'd caught nothing. Suddenly a voice said:

"Will this one do?"

Billy turned to see a monster's head raised up out of the water and a fish flapping on the rocks.

"I'm Jessica," said the monster.

"OH. . .Thank you!. . .I'm Billy. . .Can I do anything for *you*?" Jessica wanted some different food.

"I'm tired of fish," she said.

Billy raced home. He ate his supper and was back at the rock with his pockets bulging. Jessica waited.

"Come for a ride," she said, humping her back. Away they went, Billy singing at the top of his voice and Jessica beating time with her tail.

It was fun. Billy went up and down riding the monster like a rocking horse.

"I'll take you to my island," said Jessica.

Billy could see it in the distance; it looked a wonderful place. When Jessica slid up on to the beach, she lowered her back for Billy to get off. Then she surrounded him with her coiled body.

"Now Billy," she said, "what have you brought me?"

For the first time Billy noticed how beautiful she was. Her big dark eyes with thick lashes, the coloured markings on her silky skin and her gentle voice; they made her someone quite special.

"Oh, yes. . .I have. . ." he stammered. He felt he should say, 'Your Royal Highness', or 'Your Majesty!' He pulled a packet from his pocket almost ashamed of his simple gift.

"I could only bring bread. I hope you like it."

He broke a piece off and held it for her. She took it carefully, eating slowly, tasting it well.

"More, please," she asked.

Billy fed her until the last crust had gone.

"That's all, Jessica. Were you disappointed?"

She smiled: "Not at all, Billy. It was delicious!. . .What did you call it?"

Billy was delighted to have pleased her.

"Bread," he answered.

"Mmm. . .bread," she repeated. The word was new to her. Then she made him a pillow with her tail.

"There, lie down, Billy. You must be tired."

He was soon fast asleep.

Billy awoke to see eyes peeping at him over the wall of Jessica's body. These eyes belonged to crabs, lobsters, an octopus waving her arms about and a smiling dolphin. He liked the dolphin.

"They found crumbs from your bread," said Jessica. "They're hoping for some more."

Billy wished he did have more; but his pockets were empty.

"They want you to make some," went on Jessica. "In fact, they demand it."

Billy could see they were excited and quarrelsome.

"I can't!" he said. "Mother makes it!"

"Shall I bring your mother here?" Jessica whispered.

Billy shook his head. "No, she wouldn't come! Besides, she couldn't make bread here!"

Jessica was thinking.

"Would your mother make bread for me to bring back?" she asked.

"Well. . .Yes," Billy began, "if she had enough flour."

Jessica smiled. "Then my plan will work. I'll promise them bread and leave to get it. You must wait here. I'll turn back and come close in under the water. When you see my tail, jump on and we'll be away." It sounded a good idea.

"Won't they be angry and swim after us?" asked Billy.

Jessica's eyes twinkled.

"They might – but they're slow – except the dolphin and he's a friend."

She raised herself up, looked at them all and made a speech. Some clapped their claws, pleased; others grumbled. The dolphin came to stand by Billy. Jessica pushed out to sea.

"Keep them happy," advised the dolphin. "You were singing last night – start singing now."

Billy was glad to have something to do.

"I'll try," he said. His voice wouldn't come at first but soon he was braver and louder. The dolphin swayed to the music. Before long all the creatures were clapping, tapping and stamping – a real percussion band!

While they were all enjoying themselves, Jessica's tail appeared, slithering towards Billy, from the waves.

"Keep singing," muttered the dolphin, "and go – Now!"

Billy jumped – but stopped singing!

The creatures looked round.

"We've been tricked!" they cried. "You promised us bread! You promised!"

They scuttled down the beach and dived in after Jessica and Billy. Jessica outswam them all. Billy saw his mother out looking for him. He waved and shouted. How amazed she was to see him riding on the back of a monster!

He ran to her and brought her to the water's edge to meet his friend Jessica. They sat talking and Billy's mother said she would be glad to make lots of bread so that Jessica could keep her promise to the sea creatures.

Just then, who should come to join them but the dolphin. He was smiling, looking very happy. He'd persuaded the disappointed crabs, lobsters and the octopus that if only they'd be patient instead of bad tempered, everyone would be satisfied.

32

Off went Billy and his mother to get the fire going and to make the bread. They were all to meet again that evening.

What a party they had!

Jessica caught fish which Billy cooked on the beach. When his mother brought the crisp, crusty loaves there was a loud cheer. On the rocks, sat all the creatures, waiting for their share. They clapped and praised the excellent food called 'bread'. After supper they entertained one another. The dolphin gave acrobatic leaps out of the water; Billy sang and his mother told them a story.

Jessica had never enjoyed herself so much.

"Please, Billy's mother, may we come again?" she asked.

Everyone laughed and waved. "Yes, yes. . .Do please come again!"

The dolphin whispered, "She's our queen, you know."

Billy's heart bounced! "I knew it!" he muttered. . ."I just knew it!"

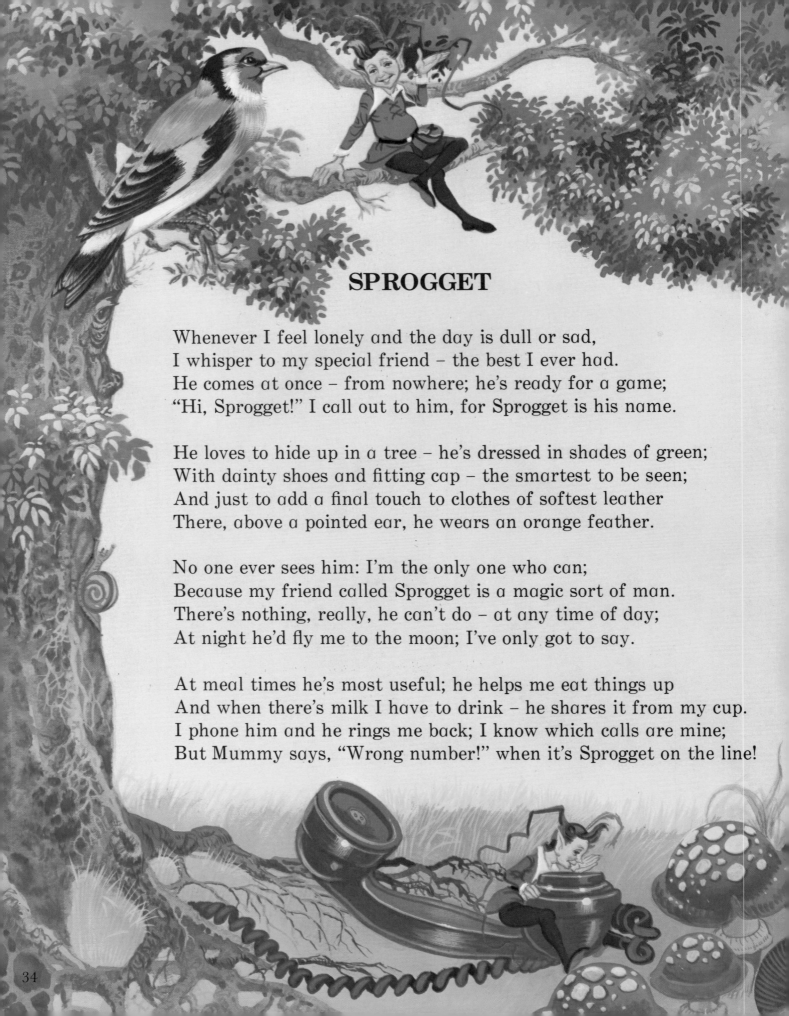

SPROGGET

Whenever I feel lonely and the day is dull or sad,
I whisper to my special friend – the best I ever had.
He comes at once – from nowhere; he's ready for a game;
"Hi, Sprogget!" I call out to him, for Sprogget is his name.

He loves to hide up in a tree – he's dressed in shades of green;
With dainty shoes and fitting cap – the smartest to be seen;
And just to add a final touch to clothes of softest leather
There, above a pointed ear, he wears an orange feather.

No one ever sees him: I'm the only one who can;
Because my friend called Sprogget is a magic sort of man.
There's nothing, really, he can't do – at any time of day;
At night he'd fly me to the moon; I've only got to say.

At meal times he's most useful; he helps me eat things up
And when there's milk I have to drink – he shares it from my cup.
I phone him and he rings me back; I know which calls are mine;
But Mummy says, "Wrong number!" when it's Sprogget on the line!

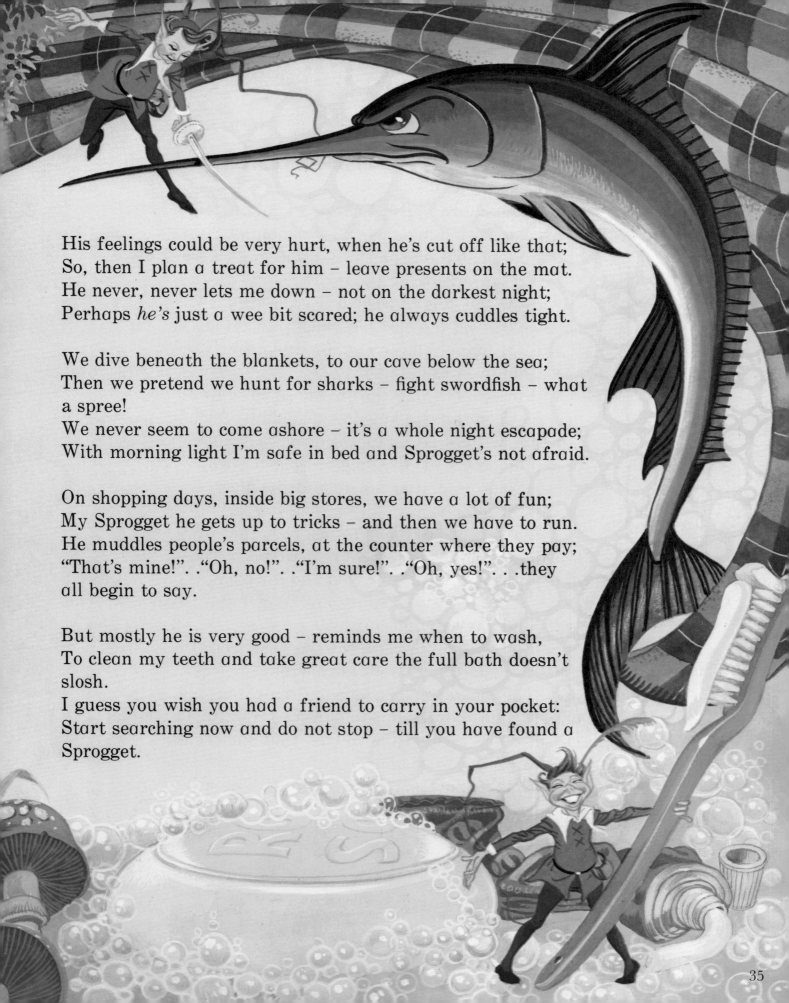

His feelings could be very hurt, when he's cut off like that;
So, then I plan a treat for him – leave presents on the mat.
He never, never lets me down – not on the darkest night;
Perhaps *he's* just a wee bit scared; he always cuddles tight.

We dive beneath the blankets, to our cave below the sea;
Then we pretend we hunt for sharks – fight swordfish – what
a spree!
We never seem to come ashore – it's a whole night escapade;
With morning light I'm safe in bed and Sprogget's not afraid.

On shopping days, inside big stores, we have a lot of fun;
My Sprogget he gets up to tricks – and then we have to run.
He muddles people's parcels, at the counter where they pay;
"That's mine!". ."Oh, no!". ."I'm sure!". ."Oh, yes!". . .they
all begin to say.

But mostly he is very good – reminds me when to wash,
To clean my teeth and take great care the full bath doesn't
slosh.
I guess you wish you had a friend to carry in your pocket:
Start searching now and do not stop – till you have found a
Sprogget.

35

THE UNEXPECTED RAINBOW

High above the earth in the land of clouds there were two kingdoms, the kingdom of Sol, and the kingdom of Splash. Both of these were ruled by powerful kings.

Now the king of Splash lived in a tall, proud castle on top of a big black rain cloud. While not many miles away, on a big, fluffy sun cloud lived the king of Sol.

You would think that living so close to one another, the two kingdoms would be friendly, but this was not so. In fact they were always quarrelling because the king of Splash always wanted it to rain, and the king of Sol always wanted it to be sunny.

So in order to make things fair, the two kingdoms agreed that one day it would be nice and sunny so that people could go for picnics, and the next, it would rain so as to give the trees and flowers a good drink.

For a time this plan worked very well, until one day things went very wrong.

The king of Splash was getting rather old, and at times he was apt to be very forgetful. His memory was getting so bad, that sometimes he even forgot to eat his breakfast.

On this particular morning, the king woke up even more forgetful than usual. He not only forgot to eat his breakfast, but he also forgot which day it was.

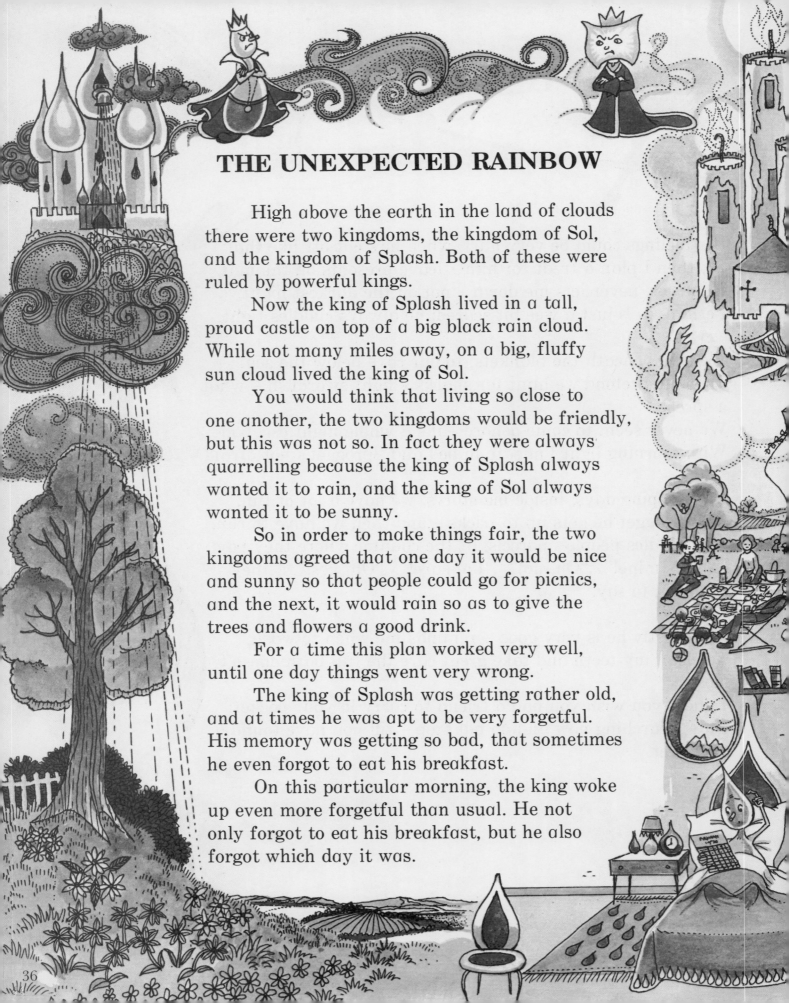

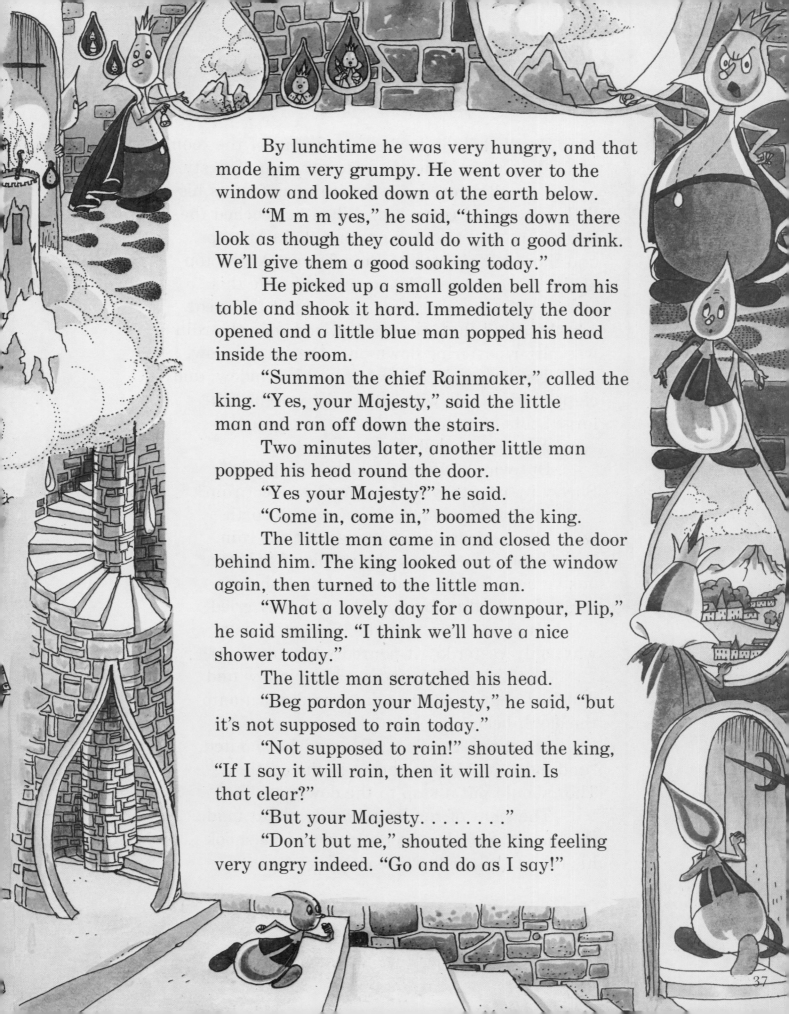

By lunchtime he was very hungry, and that made him very grumpy. He went over to the window and looked down at the earth below.

"M m m yes," he said, "things down there look as though they could do with a good drink. We'll give them a good soaking today."

He picked up a small golden bell from his table and shook it hard. Immediately the door opened and a little blue man popped his head inside the room.

"Summon the chief Rainmaker," called the king. "Yes, your Majesty," said the little man and ran off down the stairs.

Two minutes later, another little man popped his head round the door.

"Yes your Majesty?" he said.

"Come in, come in," boomed the king.

The little man came in and closed the door behind him. The king looked out of the window again, then turned to the little man.

"What a lovely day for a downpour, Plip," he said smiling. "I think we'll have a nice shower today."

The little man scratched his head.

"Beg pardon your Majesty," he said, "but it's not supposed to rain today."

"Not supposed to rain!" shouted the king, "If I say it will rain, then it will rain. Is that clear?"

"But your Majesty. . . . ."

"Don't but me," shouted the king feeling very angry indeed. "Go and do as I say!"

The little man backed slowly out of the room. "Yes, your Majesty, certainly your Majesty."

Poor Plip ran down the stairs as fast as his little legs would carry him. When he reached the bottom, he had to climb another flight of steps, and those led him to the Rain Tower. At the top of the Tower was a tiny room and inside this stood the Rainmaker. One good tug at the great wheel was all that was needed, and soon the rain was pitter-pattering down onto the earth below.

The king looked down from his window, and clapped his hands with glee as he watched the large spots of rain send the people on earth running off to find shelter.

But why had they looked so surprised? Surely by now they knew when to expect rain?

Strangely enough, the people on earth were not the only ones surprised at the rain.

A few miles away the people of Sol were gazing out of their windows in astonishment.

"Surely this could not be so," they cried.

"It is our turn to make it sunny today, why, only yesterday it poured with rain."

The king of Sol stood at his window and watched angrily as the rain poured down onto the earth below.

"Summon the Torch Bearer," he shouted, "and light the biggest candle in the castle. That should put a stop to the downpour!"

The sight of the large candle alight made the king of Splash even angrier, and he shook his fist at the great white cloud.

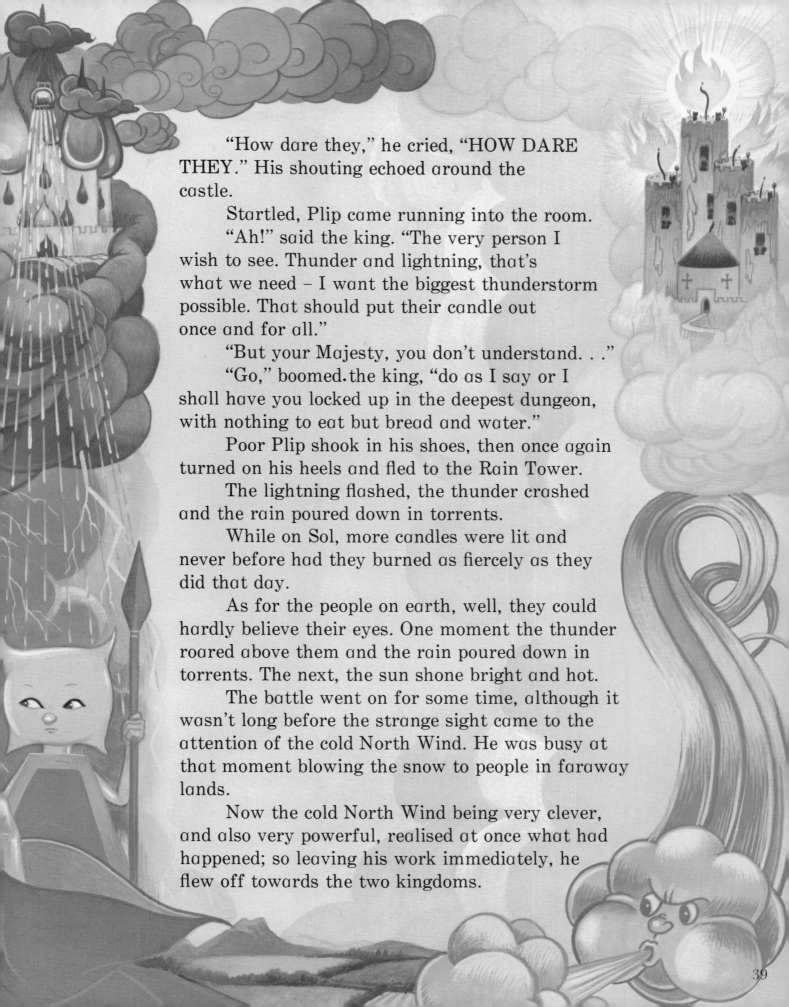

"How dare they," he cried, "HOW DARE THEY." His shouting echoed around the castle.

Startled, Plip came running into the room.

"Ah!" said the king. "The very person I wish to see. Thunder and lightning, that's what we need – I want the biggest thunderstorm possible. That should put their candle out once and for all."

"But your Majesty, you don't understand. . ."

"Go," boomed the king, "do as I say or I shall have you locked up in the deepest dungeon, with nothing to eat but bread and water."

Poor Plip shook in his shoes, then once again turned on his heels and fled to the Rain Tower.

The lightning flashed, the thunder crashed and the rain poured down in torrents.

While on Sol, more candles were lit and never before had they burned as fiercely as they did that day.

As for the people on earth, well, they could hardly believe their eyes. One moment the thunder roared above them and the rain poured down in torrents. The next, the sun shone bright and hot.

The battle went on for some time, although it wasn't long before the strange sight came to the attention of the cold North Wind. He was busy at that moment blowing the snow to people in faraway lands.

Now the cold North Wind being very clever, and also very powerful, realised at once what had happened; so leaving his work immediately, he flew off towards the two kingdoms.

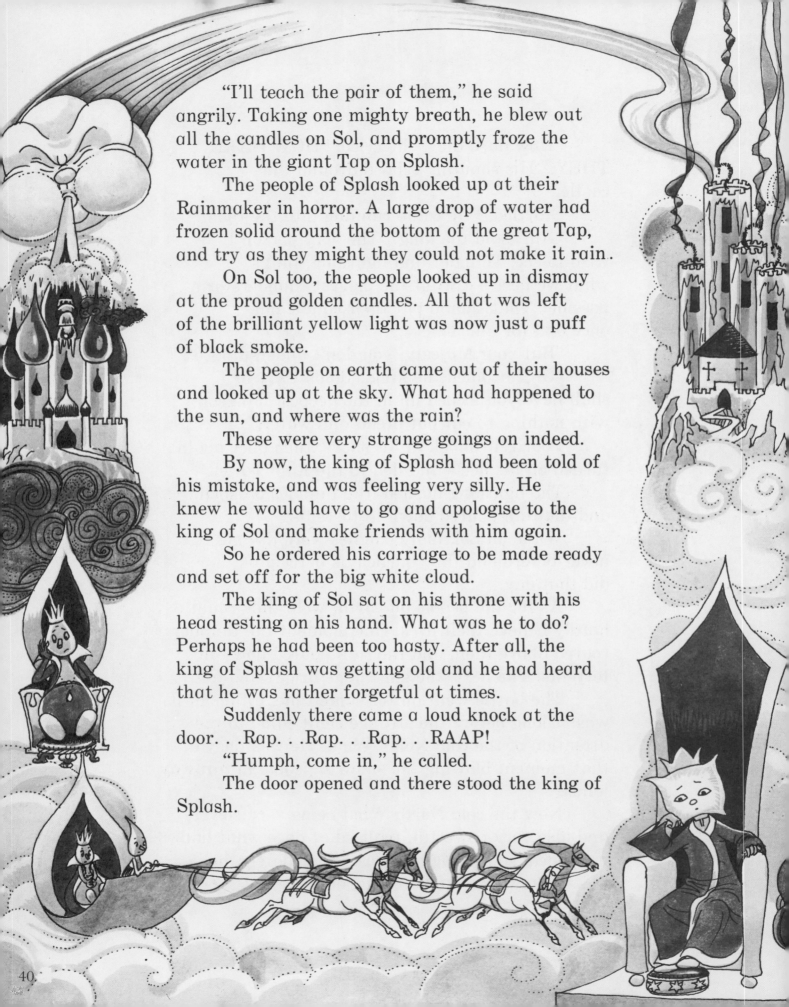

"I'll teach the pair of them," he said angrily. Taking one mighty breath, he blew out all the candles on Sol, and promptly froze the water in the giant Tap on Splash.

The people of Splash looked up at their Rainmaker in horror. A large drop of water had frozen solid around the bottom of the great Tap, and try as they might they could not make it rain.

On Sol too, the people looked up in dismay at the proud golden candles. All that was left of the brilliant yellow light was now just a puff of black smoke.

The people on earth came out of their houses and looked up at the sky. What had happened to the sun, and where was the rain?

These were very strange goings on indeed.

By now, the king of Splash had been told of his mistake, and was feeling very silly. He knew he would have to go and apologise to the king of Sol and make friends with him again.

So he ordered his carriage to be made ready and set off for the big white cloud.

The king of Sol sat on his throne with his head resting on his hand. What was he to do? Perhaps he had been too hasty. After all, the king of Splash was getting old and he had heard that he was rather forgetful at times.

Suddenly there came a loud knock at the door. . .Rap. . .Rap. . .Rap. . .RAAP!

"Humph, come in," he called.

The door opened and there stood the king of Splash.

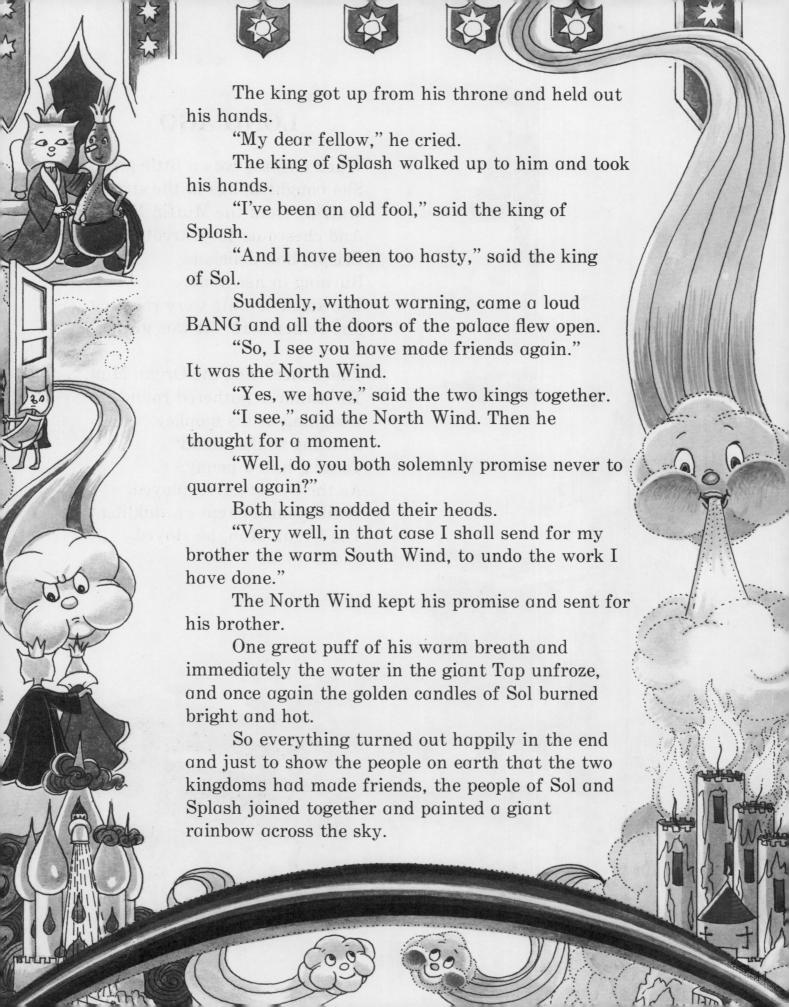

The king got up from his throne and held out his hands.

"My dear fellow," he cried.

The king of Splash walked up to him and took his hands.

"I've been an old fool," said the king of Splash.

"And I have been too hasty," said the king of Sol.

Suddenly, without warning, came a loud BANG and all the doors of the palace flew open.

"So, I see you have made friends again." It was the North Wind.

"Yes, we have," said the two kings together.

"I see," said the North Wind. Then he thought for a moment.

"Well, do you both solemnly promise never to quarrel again?"

Both kings nodded their heads.

"Very well, in that case I shall send for my brother the warm South Wind, to undo the work I have done."

The North Wind kept his promise and sent for his brother.

One great puff of his warm breath and immediately the water in the giant Tap unfroze, and once again the golden candles of Sol burned bright and hot.

So everything turned out happily in the end and just to show the people on earth that the two kingdoms had made friends, the people of Sol and Splash joined together and painted a giant rainbow across the sky.

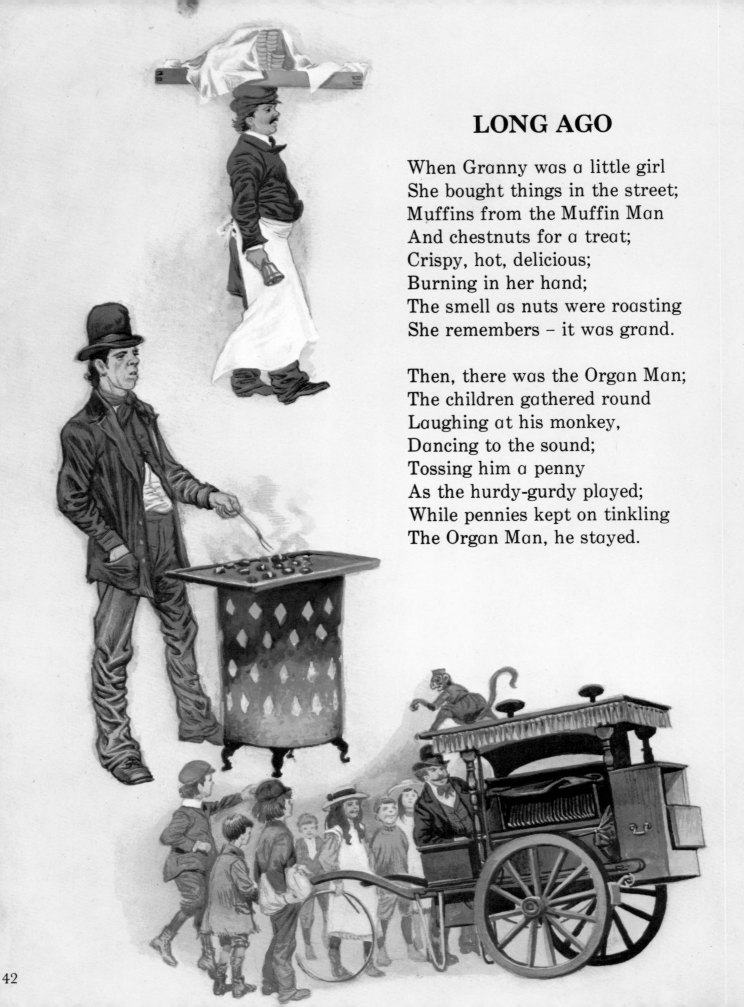

LONG AGO

When Granny was a little girl
She bought things in the street;
Muffins from the Muffin Man
And chestnuts for a treat;
Crispy, hot, delicious;
Burning in her hand;
The smell as nuts were roasting
She remembers – it was grand.

Then, there was the Organ Man;
The children gathered round
Laughing at his monkey,
Dancing to the sound;
Tossing him a penny
As the hurdy-gurdy played;
While pennies kept on tinkling
The Organ Man, he stayed.

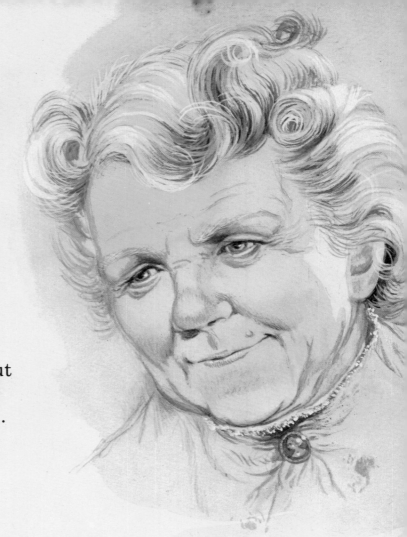

But Granny liked the man the best
With windmills on his barrow;
Reds and yellows, bright and gay
Whirring in the breeze.
"Oh Mother, Mother!" she would say,
"A jam jar, quickly please!"
Then out to change it for the toy:
To think a jar could buy such joy!

And while she played and chased about
In other streets she'd hear him shout:
"Windmills for jam jars. . .jam jars. . .
jam jars!"
Fading as he went;
And Granny was so happy
With the jam jar she had spent.

CHEESE AND BEES

"Haste away and lock the doors," shouted Martha McGimble as she ran through the village street, her hair falling from its net and the vegetables falling from her basket so great was her hurry. "Haste you away. . .the tinkers are on the road."

At the mention of tinkers everyone in the sleepy village street woke with a start.

"Quick Mary. . .lock up the chickens," shouted Mary's mother.

"Take the pig into the barn and bolt the door," shouted Daniel's father.

The women ran to take in their washing. The men gathered up their rakes and hammers. The children picked up their balls and called to their dogs.

"The tinkers are coming. . .hurry. . .hurry. . ."

Normally the village folk welcomed tinkers. The kind of tinker, that is, who sold pots and pans and stewed his dinner in an old iron pot over a kindling fire. These tinkers, the tinkers they ran from, were tinkers of a different kind. They were tinkers who stole clothes from washing lines, tinkers who broke fences and put other peoples dinners in their cooking pots and other peoples possessions in their pockets. When they were in the village nothing was safe, unless it was locked up or hidden.

The tinkers thought it a lovely joke to frighten so many people all at the same time and they were always raiding the village. Things got so bad that soon no one dared to hang washing out at all. Potatoes couldn't be dug and left to dry in the sun anymore. Chickens could no longer be allowed to peck freely in the long grass.

"Something has to be done about this," fumed Old John, when one day the tinkers crept into the village unnoticed and stole the very chair he was sitting on. "We must consult the wizard."

"Are you sure that will be safe?" asked one of Old John's friends.

"Not for those rascally tinkers I hope," said Old John.

The wizard had lived in the village for many years. The villagers always took great care not to upset him for they didn't quite know what he could do in the way of spells. But he had always been friendly and he had helped them out of trouble before, so Old John and the village elders went to consult him.

"I know why you have come," said the wizard before they could utter a word. "Turn round and go home. Next time the tinkers come to the village close your windows and lock your doors and leave the rest to me."

The village elders went home, not having said a word, but knowing somehow that the wizard understood their problem and would help.

"I can never understand how he knows things without being told," said Old John's wife. "Makes me feel kind of creepy, that does. . . ."

It made Old John feel a bit uneasy too.

But not as uneasy as the tinkers felt a few days later. They descended on the village in a noisy, rowdy band. Windows were closed and doors locked in the twinkling of an eye.

"Ha. .ha. .ha. ." laughed the tinker chief. "Someone was in such a hurry he forgot his cheese."

And indeed, standing right where the tinkers couldn't fail to see it, on a three-legged stool to raise it from the ground, was a round, ripe and beautiful cheese.

There was a lot of whispering going on behind locked doors.

"Whose cheese is that?"

"How did that cheese get there?"

47

"The cheese is mine," said the wizard hobbling from his house, pretending to be afraid. . .which he wasn't.

"Oh no it isn't. . .not any more," said the tinker chief.

"Just let me take one slice," said the wizard, quickly sinking his knife into it's creamy skin.

"Away from there!" shouted the tinker in a temper.

He roughly pushed the wizard to one side, but not before the wizard had whispered something to the cheese.

From the hole which he had just cut rose a thousand humming, buzzing, angry bees, that buzzed and threatened and stung. . .and stung. . .and stung. . .and stung. . .

"Ow . . . ow . . . ow . . ." screeched the tinkers as they took to their heels and ran, with the bees following close behind. The bees may be chasing the tinkers still because neither the bees, nor the tinkers, were ever seen in the village again.

As for the wizard, he went back to his cottage and bothered nobody, and nobody bothered him until there was another problem to solve. That way everyone was happy. Except those rascally tinkers of course.

CLACKETY CLACK

There is an old woman
Who spins in the sky.
Clackety, clackety, clack.
She spins all day long,
And all night-time too.
Clackety, clackety, clack.

She spins clouds in wisps.
She spins clouds in billows.
She spins them in sheets,
And fluffs them like pillows.
She spins puffs of white,
And blankets of grey.
She spins yellow and gold
At the end of the day.

There is an old woman
Who spins on a wheel.
Clackety, clackety, clack.
Without her the sky
Would be empty and still.
Clackety, clackety, clack.

49

THE ROLLING DRUM

Jason Brown was walking along the lane one sunny morning, wondering what he could do to pass the time, when he met a man carrying a drum. The drum was simply enormous, and the man was rather short, and Jason couldn't decide whether the pair of them looked more like a drum which had grown a head and two legs, or a man with a drum where his tummy should have been.

"Are you laughing at me?" asked the man crossly.

"Of course not," said Jason.

"It's no laughing matter when you have something as big and as awkward as this to carry," said the man.

"Then why don't you put it on a cart and push it?" asked Jason.

"Because no one will lend me a cart," said the man.

"Then put it on the ground and roll it along," said Jason.

"I've already tried that. I couldn't see where I was going. I pushed it into a tree and made a dent in it. Now stop pestering me and let me get on my way."

"I'll help you if you like," said Jason. "If you roll the drum along the road I'll walk in front and call out directions. I won't let you bump into anything . . . I promise."

The man was tired. The drum was heavy and his arms ached. He supposed it was worth a try. He lowered the drum to the ground and rubbed the stiffness from his arms.

"I've got a better idea," he said. "YOU push, and I'll guide you."

Jason didn't mind pushing. He thought it might be rather fun. So off they set, with Jason pushing and the man guiding.

"To the left . . . to the left . . ." shouted the man, dancing about all over the road like a little leprechaun. "Now . . . a little to the right . . . you're going too fast . . . you're going too slow . . . push straighter . . . mind that stone . . . look out, there's a pot-hole . . . further to the left . . . further to the right . . ."

Jason was getting confused.

"No . . . no . . . I said left . . . LOOK OUT . . . you'll hit that tree . . . can't you push straight? . . ."

"It's all very well for you . . . You can see where I'm going . . . I can't," grumbled Jason.

"Stop mumbling, boy . . . and keep pushing . . ." shouted the man excitedly. He was enjoying himself. It wasn't often he had a boy to order around. He shouted so many different instructions, so quickly, one after the other, that Jason's poor head began to spin.

Jason decided enough was enough. He stopped pushing and put his hands over his ears.

"What's this . . . what's this?" cried the man hopping all round Jason and the stationary drum. "Surely you're not tired already?"

"Of course I'm not tired . . ." said Jason, trying his hardest to be polite. "But please stop shouting at me all the time."

"If I don't shout, you won't hear me," said the man.

"If you DO shout, I won't push anymore," said Jason.

"I'll tell you what I'll do," said the man, who was enjoying himself too much to let his helper walk away. "When I want you to steer to the left, I'll bang on the left side of the drum, and when I want you to steer to the right, I'll bang on the right side of the drum. I'll have to walk backwards I know, but I'm clever enough to manage that. Now come on . . . push . . . or it will be nightfall before I reach my destination."

Off they set again and what a commotion they made. The drum rattled and bonked along over the stony road and the man banged on it's sides with a merry rat-a-tat-tat-thump-bang-bang every two seconds. Jason's head began to feel like a drum itself, and very soon he couldn't tell which side of the real drum the man was banging.

A gang of boys who had been exploring along the hedge came to see what all the noise was about, and joined their cheers to the hub-bub.

"The circus is coming . . ." they shouted.

"No it isn't . . ." shouted the man as he rat-a-tat-tatted on the drum.

A dog came from the wood where he'd been chasing rabbits and ran after them.

"Yap . . . yap . . ." barked the dog.

"Caw . . . caw . . ." joined in the rooks, who until then had been sitting quietly in the trees.

"Z.Z.Z.Z . . ." buzzed the bees, forgetting all about their empty pollen sacks.

"Eeee awwww . . ." brayed a donkey.

"Baaa . . . baaa . . ." bleated the lambs.

"Moooo . . ." mooed the cows.

Jason was so confused he didn't hear one of the boys shout a warning. Neither did anyone else for that matter.

Suddenly Jason found he wasn't pushing any more. The drum was rolling by itself . . . down hill. And it was chasing the man. It's hard enough to run backwards at the best of times and this wasn't the best of times. The man's heels caught up with his toes, his legs tied themselves into a knot, and down he fell. The drum rolled on . . . over his feet . . . over his legs . . . as it rolled over his tummy he flung his arms round it and held it tightly. It didn't stop rolling, as everyone expected it to. It carried on down the hill, with the man wrapped round it like a rubber tyre.

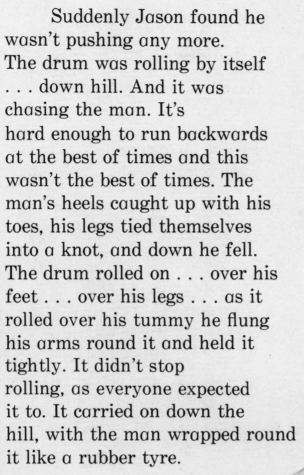

"Stop me . . . stop me . . ." he shouted. But he didn't stop until the drum stopped, and the drum didn't stop until it ran off the road at the bottom of the hill, and splashed into the duck pond.

"Quack . . . quack . . ." squawked the ducks noisily. One of them stood on top of the drum and looked down into the man's face.

"Get me out of here . . ." he shouted, "before I'm eaten alive."

Jason shooed the ducks away and the boys waded into the pond and pulled him out. Then they waded back and pulled out the drum.

"We'll push it for you mister," said the boys eagerly.

"No, you won't," shouted the man. "I don't want any more help from any more boys. I'll carry it myself."

And he did. He picked up his drum and carried it to wherever he was taking it, with water streaming from his pockets, mud squelching from his boots, and water-weed dangling from his ears. He didn't say thank you and he didn't look back once.

And Jason? He went exploring with the boys. He'd done his good deed for the day. Now it was time to have some fun.

OSCAR

A puppy named Oscar had very long ears,
They earned him unpleasant remarks, and the sneers
Of Jenny and Penny, his two lady friends,
Who swore that his ears had no shape and no ends.

He walked up and down, shedding many a tear,
And then he was struck with a splendid idea.
He went to the mirror, and with a huge grin
Tied a neat bow with them under his chin.

Now Jenny and Penny admire his good features,
They think him the very divinest of creatures.
And all the young dogs are a-wearing of bows
On ear, and on chin, and on tail, and on nose.

FIT FOR A KING

"Wife. . ." said Samuel Duggett one fine Spring morning. "I'm going to the market today to sell the white mare."

"Then be sure to get a good price for her," said his wife. "She's a beautiful horse, fit for a king to ride upon."

The way to the market led through the wood. Sam Duggett sat high on the mare's back and felt like a king himself as he jogged along through the dappled sunlight. Deep in the wood, where the brambles were most tangled and the shadows the deepest, he was hailed by an old man with a long white beard.

"Will you stop a moment? I have something to ask you."

"Whoa there, my beauty!" called Sam to the white mare. She stopped, with a soft whinny, before he even had time to tighten his grip on the bridle.

"Hallo old man. Is there something I can do for you?" asked Sam, his cheerful voice echoing through the wood like a rumble of muffled thunder.

The old man's voice was quiet. but surprisingly strong in one who looked so frail and old.

"You have a beautiful mare," he said, fondling the mare's muzzle. "If she is for sale, I will buy her."

Sam took one look at the old man's homespun robe with the worn elbows and another at his dusty feet, and laughed long and heartily.

"She is for sale, but not to the likes of you, I'm afraid. I'm taking her to market for some fine gentleman to buy. She will fetch me a very good price, of that I am sure."

And with that, he doffed his cap, bid the old man a courteous goodbye, and galloped off.

The old man watched the dust flying from the horse's hoofs and said no more, but he smiled quietly as though there was a secret which only he knew.

The market was crowded and business was good that fresh Spring morning. There were many fine gentlemen about in their tailored coats and silk cravats. Several indeed, were looking for a fine horse to buy.

Everyone, even those who wanted to buy pigs, and cows, and sacks of grain, admired Sam Duggett's fine white mare.

"She really is a beauty, Sam."

"She's magnificent. Haven't seen a mare like her for years."

Sam rubbed his hands and thought of the gold he would be taking home to his wife.

"Who is going to have the privilege of buying my lovely mare?" he asked.

But the day came, and the day went. The market filled and the market emptied.

"What . . . not sold that mare yet?" asked a man who had sold every one of his pigs.

"I don't understand it," said Sam. "You can see for yourself what a beauty she is. I've nearly sold her a dozen times . . . but nearly isn't good enough . . ."

"She's too beautiful . . . that's her trouble," said the man who had sold every pig. "I should take her home again if I were you."

That was all Sam could do. The market place was empty, there was no point in staying any longer.

He took the mare's bridle in his hand and began the slow walk home. He wanted to delay the moment when he would meet his wife for as long as possible. He knew she would scold him and say it was his fault the mare wasn't sold. To his surprise, as he was passing through the wood he met the old man again.

"I see you still have your white mare," said the old man. "Come with me, if you please."

Sam was so miserable and so anxious not to get home too soon, that he followed the old man with no argument at all. He didn't even bother to ask where they were going, or why.

After a few minutes they came to a sandstone cliff. As far as Sam could see there was no path up it, over it, or round it. Before he had time to ask any of the many questions which suddenly popped into his head, the old man struck the cliff with his fist.

Before Sam could laugh, and say, as was in his mind, "You'll never move a cliff that way, old man," two enormous gates appeared and flew open with a thunderous noise that sent the birds screeching into the sky, and the rabbits hopping to their burrows.

The old man beckoned Sam forward. Now, feeling very frightened indeed, so frightened that he was afraid not to do as the old man asked, Sam followed him into the cave which lay behind the gates.

An unbelievable sight met his eyes. King Arthur of the Round Table, and his Knights, lay sleeping in the darkness.

"King Arthur and his Knights will sleep for a long time yet," said the old man, who, it seemed to Sam, had suddenly grown very tall and straight, "but the day will come when England has need of her Ancient Kings, and then King Arthur and his Knights will wake and ride forth to battle on white horses. They need one more

·white horse . . . a horse fit for a king to ride upon . . . now . . . will you sell me your white mare?"

    Sam Duggett didn't say a word. He handed the mare's bridle to Merlin, for the old man was indeed, Merlin, the Wizard who had lived at the Court of King Arthur and who now kept watch over him as he slept. He took the purse of gold which Merlin gave him . . .
. . . and ran.

63

At the entrance to the cave, he turned for a moment. He saw Merlin leading the white mare into the darkness, and then he found he had his nose pressed against the golden coloured stone of the sandstone cliff. No one believed his story, of course. The sandstone cliff still stood in the wood but no amount of banging and thumping ever made the gates reappear. In time Sam himself found it hard to believe what had happened. But, there was one thing of which everyone was certain; the white mare had vanished, without trace.

NONSENSE

Jane's umbrella blew inside out
And lifted her up from the ground.
"I'll send you a postcard,"
She said with a shout.
"When I know where I am, when I'm found."

A BUSY BUZZING BUMBLE BEE

A busy, buzzing, bumble bee,
Came buzzing very close to me.
I stood quite still so he could see
I would not hurt him. No Siree!
I looked at him. He looked at me.
I wasn't afraid. And neither was he.
He flew around and looked me over.
It was easy to see I wasn't clover.
He buzzed around then flew away.
Perhaps we'll meet another day.

THE DRAGON OF WANTLEY

The Dragon of Wantley lay sleeping in his rocky den. From time to time, a puff of smoke came floating from his bright green nostrils, but apart from that, he was completely still. The only noise came from the dragon's pet white mouse, Wilfred, who was putting coal on the fire to make a hot breakfast for the dragon. The entrance to the dragon's coal-mine stood nearby.

As soon as the fire was glowing hot, Wilfred seized a grey goose's feather and began to tickle the dragon's nose. "Time to wake up, master," he called.

With a great fiery sneeze the Dragon of Wantley woke up. He yawned a little, stretched his legs and flapped his great wings.

"Is it breakfast time, Wilfred?" he asked, sniffing the smoke from the fire.

"Yes, master. Eat up while the coal is still hot."

The dragon began to tuck into the glowing coals with a hearty appetite. He liked hot coals for breakfast – dark smouldering red. When he had finished, he went down to the stream for a long drink of water so that he would be able to make plenty of steam during the day. Finally, he reached for the morning paper, which Wilfred had laid out carefully for him on a rock.

"Same old news, I suppose," he said, with another yawn.

The newspaper contained many reports of battles between various kings who lived in the land. The dragon glanced at the reports without paying much attention to them.

"I see the King of Noke has beaten the King of Bagby," he said. Wilfred did not answer because he was busy with a nice piece of cheese. Then, the dragon's eye was caught by a small paragraph which told how a terrible deed had been done by the wicked Black Knight. Not content with stealing all the King's gold, the Black Knight had carried off the Princess of Stoke Poges to his castle in the forest.

At once the dragon began to read more carefully, because he was a kindly dragon, who was always rescuing princesses and restoring gold to kings who had lost it.

'The princess,' said the newspaper, 'was on her way to be married to the Prince of Nether Stowey when the Black Knight rushed out of his castle and carried her off. The King of Stoke Poges has offered a reward of half his kingdom to anyone who rescues the princess.'

'Half a kingdom,' said the dragon to himself. 'That is not much of a reward for rescuing a princess. But as I never ask for a reward, I suppose it doesn't matter.'

As soon as Wilfred had finished with his cheese, the dragon called out to him. "Wilfred," he said, "we are going to Stoke Poges to rescue another princess. You had better climb on my back."

"I hope she is beautiful," said Wilfred.

"Of course she is," replied the dragon. "All princesses are beautiful."

Wilfred ran along the dragon's scaly tail until he came to his favourite perch, just between the dragon's pointed ears. With a great swish of his wings, the dragon rose into the air and set his course by the sun for Stoke Poges.

Below them as they flew through the air they could see the many towns and villages of England, all with their kings and castles. Some of the castles were being besieged, and in other places, the kings were fighting each other with great armies. But the Dragon of Wantley flew steadily on his course through the sky. A great many people who were not fighting came out to see him go by, but as they had been taught that dragons did not exist, they refused to believe what they saw.

At last, just after one o'clock, the dragon arrived at Stoke Poges. They went straight to the castle to see the king, who was having his lunch. The dragon and Wilfred bowed before the royal throne.

"I have come to rescue the princess and restore your gold, sire," said the dragon. The king looked extremely pleased.

"Thank you, my boy," he said. "I hope you will have some lunch first."

"Certainly, sire," replied the dragon. "I will have a little fresh coal if I may. My mouse would like some cheese if you have any."

The king clapped his hands. Immediately the royal servants brought in a hundred sacks of coal and a huge block of cheese for the guests. While they ate, the king explained the way to the Black Knight's castle.

"If you take the road into the forest," said the king, "you will see the Black Knight's castle on the left as you go past the thousandth oak tree. Knock on the gate and state your business. He will then come out to fight with you, and may the best man win."

"Thank you, sire," said the dragon. "I will be on my way now, if I may."

"By all means, my boy," said the king. "I will see you to the door."

Wilfred climbed back between the dragon's ears and they left the castle, taking the forest road as instructed.

69

"Let us both count the oak trees," said the dragon, "to make sure
we do not miss the castle."

They set off through the forest. At the thousandth oak tree, the
dragon stopped.

"How many oak trees have you counted?" he asked.

"Eight hundred and sixty four," replied Wilfred.

"I see," said the dragon. "We had better begin again."

They went back to the edge of the forest and began to count again.
For the second time they counted differently, and once more they went
back to the beginning. The third time they managed to agree on
the thousandth oak tree, and there, sure enough, was the castle on the
left. The dragon marched up to it boldly and knocked at the gate.

"Who goes there?" cried a gruff voice.

"The Dragon of Wantley. I have come to rescue the Princess of
Stoke Poges and return the gold you have stolen from her father."

"Wait there a moment while I fetch my armour," answered the gruff
voice.

After a delay of about ten minutes, the Black Knight charged over the drawbridge of his castle on a magnificent black horse. He lowered his lance and began to gallop towards the dragon, who knew exactly how to deal with a situation like this.

When the knight was almost close enough to touch, the dragon let out a small flame with a big puff of smoke. At once the knight pulled up in amazement.

"Where is your lance?" he shouted. "I cannot fight you unless you have a lance, or at least a sword."

For reply, the Dragon of Wantley simply let out a long stream of flame.

"This is disgraceful," shouted the knight. "Fight properly or not at all!"

Once again the dragon let out a flame. Then he made a terrible roar which frightened the knight's horse. The horse ran away, taking the knight with him.

"Well done, master," said Wilfred. "He will not return yet."

"I don't understand why he was so frightened of me," said the dragon. "I would never hurt him, no matter how many princesses he had captured."

They went into the castle and found the dungeon where the princess was kept. The dragon burnt down the door with a long flame, and out stepped the princess. To their amazement, she was not beautiful at all. In fact, she was fat and rather ugly with ordinary brown hair. However, the dragon bowed low just the same.

"I have come to save you from the Black Knight," he said.

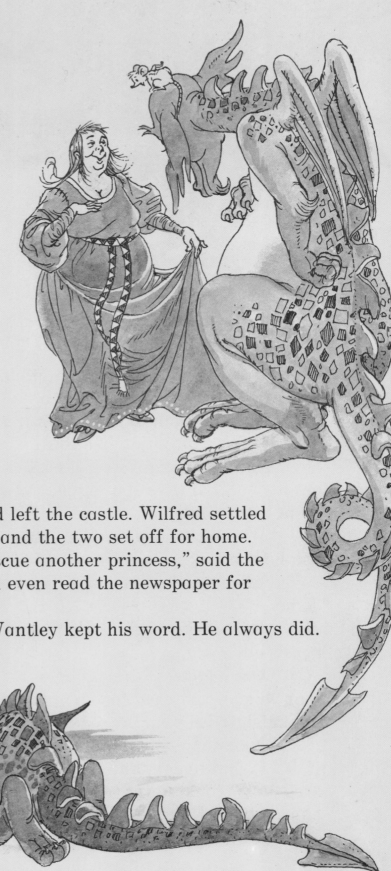

"There was no need to bother," replied the princess. "I do not want to be rescued at all. If I am rescued, I shall have to marry the horrid Prince of Nether Stowey. Please let me stay here."

The dragon could see that the fat princess would cry if he carried her back to the king, so he decided to leave her with the Black Knight after all.

"Would you like me to rescue your father's gold?" he asked.

"No, thank you," she replied. "It is not real gold. It is only painted wood. My father would never let anyone steal his real gold."

The dragon gave a low bow and left the castle. Wilfred settled down comfortably between his ears, and the two set off for home.

"I shall think twice before I rescue another princess," said the dragon. "In fact, I don't think I shall even read the newspaper for weeks and weeks."

What is more, the Dragon of Wantley kept his word. He always did.

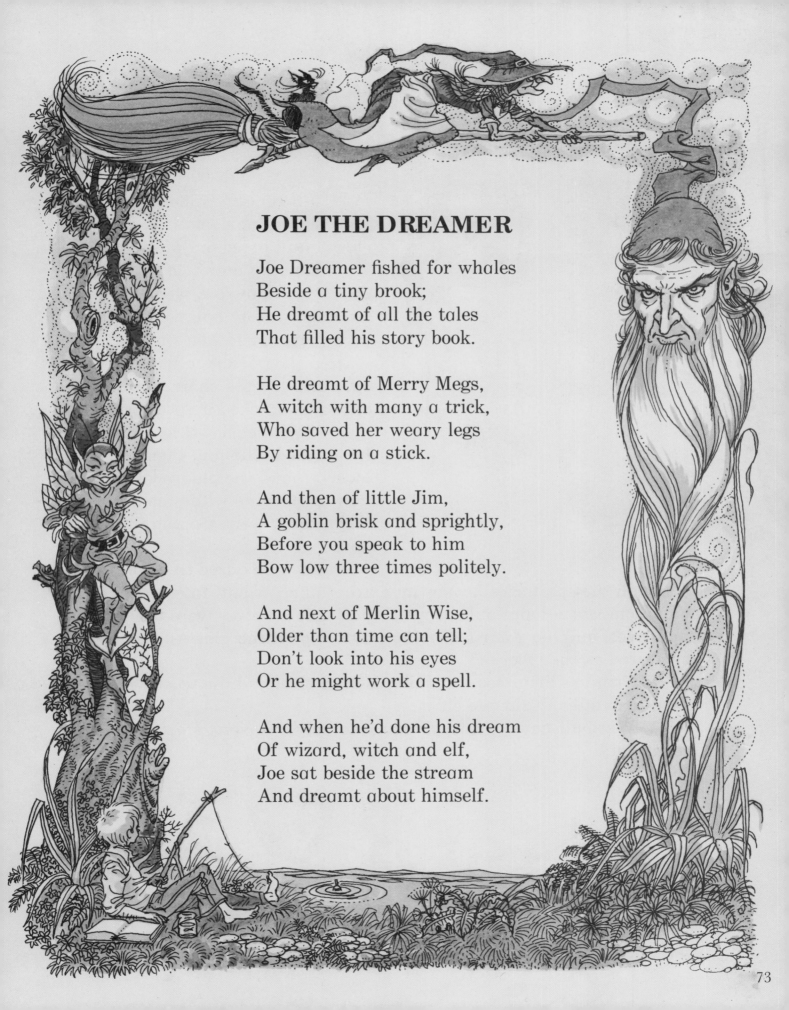

JOE THE DREAMER

Joe Dreamer fished for whales
Beside a tiny brook;
He dreamt of all the tales
That filled his story book.

He dreamt of Merry Megs,
A witch with many a trick,
Who saved her weary legs
By riding on a stick.

And then of little Jim,
A goblin brisk and sprightly,
Before you speak to him
Bow low three times politely.

And next of Merlin Wise,
Older than time can tell;
Don't look into his eyes
Or he might work a spell.

And when he'd done his dream
Of wizard, witch and elf,
Joe sat beside the stream
And dreamt about himself.

THE MAGIC SPECTACLES

"Goodnight, Timothy!" Grandpa finished telling Timothy a bedtime story and tiptoed out of the room.

Timothy didn't go to sleep at once. He lay awake, wondering how Grandpa was able to make up so many lovely bedtime stories. Then he noticed that Grandpa had left his spectacles on the chair. He slipped out of bed and picked up the spectacles.

"I wonder how I look in them," he laughed. Slipping them on, he looked round the playroom, in which he was sleeping while his grandpa and granny were staying in the house.

Then he gazed in astonishment. Through the spectacles he saw an extraordinary sight. In a corner of the playroom was a long table at which half a dozen elves were busy cutting up loaves, making pastry, stirring bowls and fitting glasses. They chattered as they worked.

"Princess Primrose's wedding is at twelve, and the feast will begin very soon after," said one elf.

"We shall have to hurry," said another. "I haven't started icing the cakes yet."

Timothy could hear sounds outside, so he opened the playroom door, which led into the garden. Outside he could see people everywhere, little people. None of them was higher than his knee. There were gnomes too, and fairies at gaily decorated stalls full of flags and streamers. Children were dressed in their best clothes; flags and bunting decorated the streets. Above the main street rose a beautiful glass palace, with a red carpet laid along the courtyard in front. Uniformed soldiers paced to and fro before the steps.

Suddenly a great commotion arose. A bell rang out. It belonged to the Town Crier, who called out startling news. The handsome prince bridegroom could not get to the city to marry Princess Primrose at twelve o'clock. He was travelling by train from a far country, and wicked goblins had broken down the bridge between his country and the Land of Makebelieve, so that the train with all his guests could not cross the wide river.

Cries of dismay went up from all the people, and children began to cry.

'In the stories Grandpa tells me,' said Timothy to himself, 'goblins are always getting up to mischief.'

He knew there was a stream at the far end of his daddy's garden. Perhaps to tiny folk and gnomes and fairies, the stream would be a wide river. He would go and see!

He soon reached the stream. Sure enough, there was a train – a toy train to him – standing still on the other side of the stream. It couldn't go any farther. The wooden bridge over the water was wrecked. Stooping, Timothy lifted the little train, with all the people in it, over the stream and set it carefully on the rail on his side. Faces appeared at the windows of the train and arms waved. The train puffed happily away to the cheers of the passengers.

Timothy reached the city again before the train. He heard the Town Crier ring his bell and call out that news had come through that a kind giant had lifted the train over the wide river, and that the bridegroom was on his way to the wedding. The people cheered, the children waved their flags, and the band struck up rousing music.

When the train arrived, the handsome prince stepped out, and a troop of soldiers on horseback rode up to escort him to the church. But first the bride had to walk from the palace to the church. As the church bells rang out, she stepped down the palace stairs on the arm of her father, the King. She was about the step on to the red carpet when a dreadful thing happened. Rain began to fall in torrents. It came out of a clear sky. Princess Primrose shrank back. People ran for shelter. Nobody had an umbrella and it looked as if everybody would be soaked to the skin.

But Timothy saw what was happening. He ran to the far wall of the garden. A dozen goblins, chortling with glee, were holding a water hose which was attached to a tap in the wall. The goblins had climbed on each other's shoulders and turned on the tap. Now they were sending the water up in the air and over all the people.

"Stop it!" cried Timothy.

He grabbed the hose, but he didn't turn the water off. Instead, he turned it on the goblins, who ran away shouting and screaming angrily. They were soon wet through.

"I don't think we shall see them again today!" chuckled Timothy.
Turning the tap off, he hurried back. He was just in time to see
Princess Primrose walk along the red carpet to the church, with the
children waving their flags and cheering.

'Why,' thought Timothy, 'Princess Primrose looks just like my
sister's bride-doll!'

He stooped down to try to peer into the church, but the spectacles fell from his nose – and suddenly, the whole scene had gone! He was looking on the garden just as it had always been. Then he heard the voice of Grandpa, who had come in search of his spectacles.

"Ah, there you are, Timothy! Good! You've found my spectacles. Come back to bed now, there's a good boy."

As he tucked Timothy into bed, he said, "I won't tell you another story tonight, as it is getting late."

Timothy nodded and yawned. "I don't want another tonight," he murmured. "I've just been in one."

NED OF THE TODDIN AGAIN

Ned of the Toddin was a very unusual ginger kitten. He lived on an emerald green bank between an old stone farmhouse and a brambly wood. His mother's name was Waowhler, and his father's name was Skaratch. His round eyes sparkled with curiosity, because all cats are curious, as you know.

One day, Ned went out towards the brambly wood to catch a mouse for his dinner. He went down the emerald green bank, across the field, and into the bramble bushes. They didn't scratch him because he was so small. Now he hadn't gone very far when he heard a noise. PID A PAD. PID A PAD. Just like that. Round the corner came a big black cat. His coat was black, his nose was black, and his whiskers were black. His eyes gleamed like little bonfires. His name was Clawface The Magnificent, and he was the most dreaded cat in all the neighbourhood.

"Out of my way, little kitten," said Clawface the Magnificent. "This is my brambly wood. You have no business to be here."

"No, I won't get out of the way," said Ned. "I am looking for my dinner."

"Go home to your mother at once," said Clawface, "or I'll have you for MY dinner."

"No, I won't," said Ned, who wasn't afraid of anybody.

"MIAAAAAAAOUW!" cried Clawface The Magnificent. "Do as you're told or I'll spank you hard."

"If you do," said Ned, "I'll crumple your whiskers with my twitchy tail."

Now, Clawface was not used to being spoken to like that by a little kitten. Without more ado he sprang towards Ned, and he would certainly have spanked him very hard indeed, but Ned turned round and hit him on the nose with his twitchy tail. PLONK. Just like that. Clawface The Magnificent became so angry he didn't know what to do. His black fur stood on end, his black tail waved about, and he hissed. SSSSSSSS!

But Ned of the Toddin sat very calmly and licked his furry paws, for all the world as if there was nothing going on at all.

Suddenly, Clawface the Magnificent sprang again, but Ned jumped out of the way at once. Then he caught hold of poor Clawface's front legs with his twitchy tail. He pulled Clawface's legs hard, and Clawface fell on his nose in a patch of damp grass.

"SSSSS!" he said, "SSSSSSS!"

Ned left Clawface where he was, and went on his way to look for his dinner. He had not gone far when he heard a rustling noise coming from the wavy corn. Before he knew where he was, there stood a brown hare. The hare had long ears, long back legs, and little short front legs. His name was Mauleverer Hopquick. He was the fastest hare in all the neighbourhood.

"Hallo little kitten," said Mauleverer Hopquick. "Would you like a race round the field?"

"If you like," said Ned.

"I bet you can't run as fast as I can," said Mauleverer Hopquick. So, I will give you a start."

But before he had time to say any more, Ned was off. He ran round the field so fast you couldn't see his legs at all, and although Mauleverer Hopquick ran as fast as he could, he could not catch up with him.

"That wasn't fair, little kitten," said Mauleverer. "You didn't wait for me to start. This time I will count."

So Mauleverer Hopquick counted. ONE, TWO, THREE! Just like that. Yet, although he ran faster than he had ever run before, he could not catch up with furry Ned. Round and round the field they went, and I'm afraid they knocked over a great many ears of corn,

until poor Mauleverer sat down under a shady tree.

"Phew!" he cried. "I didn't know kittens could run as fast as that."

"Some of them can," said Ned. He began to wash his whiskers, for all the world as if he had just been out for a walk in the dappled sunshine.

They had not been sitting there long when they heard a strange noise. H.H.H.H.H.H.H.H! Just like that. As soon as they heard it, they knew there was a dog coming. H.H.H.H.H! The noise came nearer and nearer until it was just behind the shady tree.

"Goodbye, little kitten," said Mauleverer Hopquick. "I must be off." He ran across the field like greased lightning, which as you know is very fast indeed.

H.H.H.H! The noise came right round the tree, and there stood an enormous dog. He had sharp teeth, sharp ears, a sharp nose and sharp claws. His name was Woofus Woofusson. He was the fiercest dog for miles.

"RRRRR," he said. "Little kitten I'm going to bite your tail off."

"Oh, no, you're not," said Ned.

Quick as a flash, he jumped onto Woofus Woofusson's back. There he sat, and although Woofus Woofusson danced about, and did everything he could think of to get him down, he simply stayed there, for all the world as if he were stuck on with glue.

"Come off my back, little kitten," cried Woofus Woofusson, "and I'll let you go home to your mother."

Now, furry Ned knew he wouldn't do anything of the sort, but he jumped nimbly down, and started to walk away. Woofus Woofusson came after him immediately to try to bite him, but Ned caught hold of his collar with his twitchy tail and threw him high into the branches of a shady tree. His leather collar caught on a twig, and he hung there, gently swaying to and fro in the breeze.

"Rrrr," he said, feeling very sorry for himself. Just then Woofus's master came by on his way to the old stone farmhouse.

"You're in a fine state, aren't you my lad?" he said.

Woofus's master reached up to the tree to get Woofus down. As he put his arms up, something fell out of his pocket. It was a packet of CHEESE SANDWICHES.

As soon as Woofus and his master had gone on their way to the farmhouse Ned ran up to the sandwiches. He undid the packet with his twitchy tail and ate them up for his dinner. MUNCH. MUNCH. MUNCH. Just like that.

"I do like cheese sandwiches," said Ned.

Then, because he had eaten his dinner, he lay down in a patch of warm sunshine and fell fast asleep, for all the world like an ordinary little kitten who had never even heard of cheese.

"PRRRRR," he said. "PRRRRR."

HUMPTY DUMPTY

Humpty Dumpty climbed over the wall;
He'd really no business there at all;
He cut his hand,
He tore his trews
And scuffed the toes of his newest shoes.

He slithered down onto grassy ground
Then brushed himself off and looked around;
Soldiers approached
And grabbed at him:
"Young man, you must come and see the King!"

They marched him then to the High Court room;
He trembled to think upon his doom;
The King looked up,
Eyes opened wide,
He laughed and laughed till he almost cried.

"Pray, what on earth do you call yourself?
Should you not be on the dairy shelf?
Aren't you an egg
Fresh laid· – surely?
And for heaven's sake, why come to me!"

At the name, 'Humpty Dumpty', the King
Laughed again: "You're an 'eggstra' strange thing;
A mascot, eh?
To cheer my men!
Clean him up and I'll see him again."

Humpty was dressed in uniform fine
And there he marched at the head of the line.
When he was tired
They held him up
And bore him along in the King's egg-cup.

His fame it spread wide from land to land;
He'd a special tune and a special band;
Such special care
They had to take
For never; oh, never, must Humpty break!

WHY WINTER WAS LATE ONE YEAR

The East Wind had a cold. He should have stayed in bed of course, but the East Wind was very stubborn and once he had made up his mind about something, nothing and nobody could change it for him. Or so he thought.

"I haven't been out to blow for weeks," he complained to North, South and West, who were doing their best to make him stay in bed. "Every time I go out to make the leaves shiver and the ponds freeze, one of you has got there before me. If I don't start blowing soon Old Man Winter will never wake up."

"One more day of sleep won't hurt him," said South Wind, trying to push him back into bed.

"Take your hands off me . . . you . . . you . . . warm wind you! . . ." snapped East Wind, with more than a hint of ice in his voice.

"At least put your scarf on," said West Wind and began to wind yards and yards of striped scarf round East Wind's neck, and yards and yards more of the same scarf, which was very long indeed, round East Wind's middle, and then the rest of it round his ears. The scarf was so long it stretched further than the eye could see when it was laid out straight. and when it was all wrapped round East Wind, his nose, his toes, and his knobbly knees, were the only parts of him which showed.

"How do you expect me to blow properly with this . . . this thing, wrapped round my person?" snapped East Wind icily.

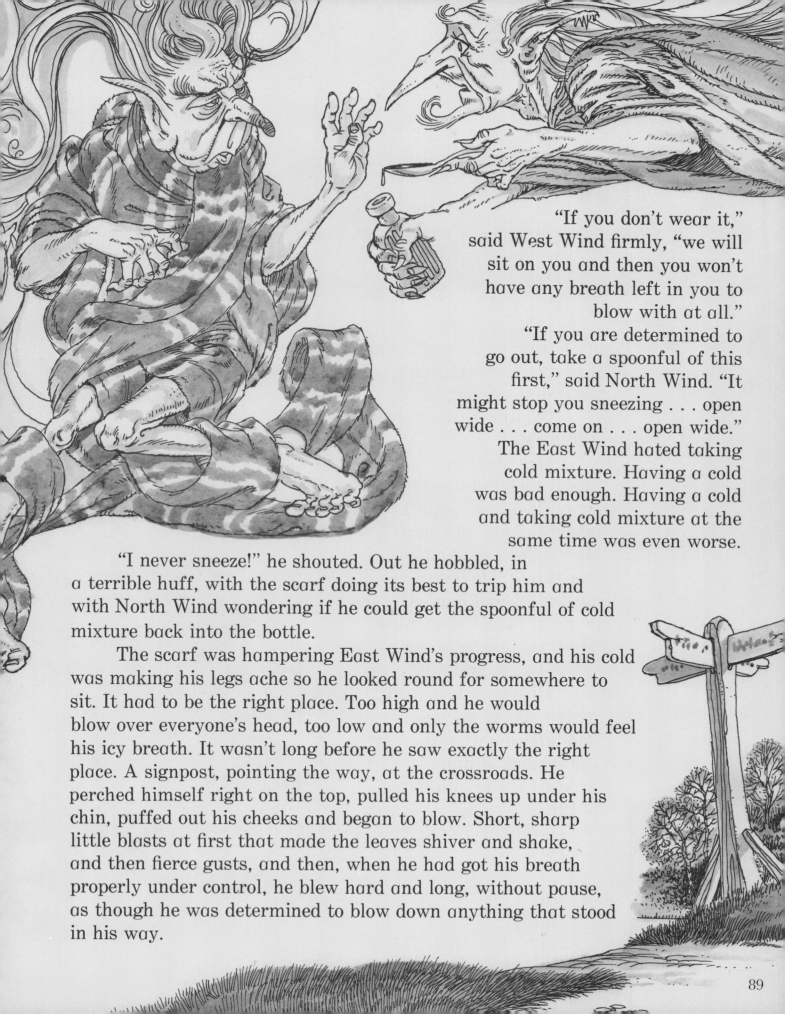

"If you don't wear it," said West Wind firmly, "we will sit on you and then you won't have any breath left in you to blow with at all."

"If you are determined to go out, take a spoonful of this first," said North Wind. "It might stop you sneezing . . . open wide . . . come on . . . open wide."

The East Wind hated taking cold mixture. Having a cold was bad enough. Having a cold and taking cold mixture at the same time was even worse.

"I never sneeze!" he shouted. Out he hobbled, in a terrible huff, with the scarf doing its best to trip him and with North Wind wondering if he could get the spoonful of cold mixture back into the bottle.

The scarf was hampering East Wind's progress, and his cold was making his legs ache so he looked round for somewhere to sit. It had to be the right place. Too high and he would blow over everyone's head, too low and only the worms would feel his icy breath. It wasn't long before he saw exactly the right place. A signpost, pointing the way, at the crossroads. He perched himself right on the top, pulled his knees up under his chin, puffed out his cheeks and began to blow. Short, sharp little blasts at first that made the leaves shiver and shake, and then fierce gusts, and then, when he had got his breath properly under control, he blew hard and long, without pause, as though he was determined to blow down anything that stood in his way.

"Brr, what an icy wind! It is getting cold," said the people passing by.

"Wouldn't be surprised if it snows."

That was the kind of talk East Wind liked to hear. He almost smiled, in spite of his cold and his tickling nose and his sore throat. He blew harder . . . and harder . . . and then . . . he did something which he said he never did do . . . he sneezed.

He sneezed so hard, he fell off the signpost and landed with a thud on the ground. It quite knocked the breath out of him.

"Thank goodness that nasty East Wind has dropped," said people passing by. "And what a good thing too!"

Now that was the kind of talk the East Wind didn't like to hear.

"I'll show them . . . I'll make them complain," he grumbled. He climbed back onto the signpost, pulled up his knees, loosened his scarf and got ready to blow the longest, iciest, meanest blow, he'd ever blown. He was so cross he failed to notice that the end of his scarf was coming unwound and that yards and yards of it were already dangling beside the signpost. He blew harder, and harder still. His breath was white, and frosty with ice. The loose end of his scarf somehow got caught in the lash of his breath and it began to wind itself round and round the signpost.

91

There was already a layer of ice on the ponds.

"Brrr . . . winter's on its way . . ." shivered people as they hurried past.

The East Wind blew harder and harder . . . until he did, again, what he said he never did do. He sneezed. It was such a sudden, jerky sneeze, it tugged the end of the scarf which was wound round the signpost and started to unwind it. Once it started to unwind it would not . . . could not . . . stop.

It spun the signpost round just like a spinning top. Round and round and round. Quicker and quicker and quicker, till it was just a whizzing blur. The East Wind, who was spinning round too, and whose breath was spinning round inside him, was so surprised and confused he forgot to stop blowing.

Hats blew into the air in spirals, and everything that could move was blown first in one direction and then in another.

"What's happened to the wind? It's gone mad!" cried the people, with so many bumps and collisions and narrow misses going on round their ears.

The signpost continued it's crazy twirl until the scarf had completely unwound, and then it wobbled to a stop. East Wind immediately lost his balance and fell to the ground. He lay there, waiting for his breath to stop spinning inside him and thought about the advice his friends had given him.

"They were quite right. I should have stayed in bed. I should have taken the cold mixture," he said. "I shall go home and I shall stay in bed until I'm better. Winter will have to sleep a little longer this year."

And that is exactly what he did do, leaving some very puzzled people and a very wobbly signpost behind him.

Ever after that, whenever the East Wind blew, the signpost at the crossroads got confused and spun round and round on the spot like a spinning top. It was always sending people off in the wrong direction and getting the blame for something which wasn't really its fault.

CHUFFA'S MOON TRIP

Chuffa the engine is cheerful, chunky and charming. He is also
dozy, dreamy and drowsy. Here he is at the end of the line, dozing in
the silvery moonlight. And there on his funnel is Sebastian, the
seagull who is one of Chuffa's best friends. Sebastian thinks he would
like to be like Chuffa – sturdy, steely, strong and hardworking and only
sometimes late. And Chuffa thinks he would like to be like Sebastian –
flying, floating, skimming and swooping through the air. If only he,
Chuffa, could fly. He dreams of flying like a bird – like Sebastian.
He gives a big sigh, CH-uff, and dozes off to sleep.

Suddenly he hears Sebastian calling. Not just one Sebastian, but six Sebastians! Why they are lifting Chuffa up into the air. All six of them. How strong they are. Well, Sebastian always wanted to be strong, didn't he? And here he is making Chuffa's dreams come true – making Chuffa fly like a bird in the sky. Chuffa looks down and sees the whole world and one sleepy squirrel all silvery in the moonlight, while they soar up into the air.

Chuffa is not the least bit afraid even when they have left the earth far, far behind and are up in Cloud-land where the cherubs and the angels live in the clouds.

But even six strong Sebastians cannot go on lifting up a Chuffa engine without getting rather tired. There is even a danger that they might drop Chuffa! Oh, how terrible that would be! So Sebastian asks help from two dear little angels sitting on a golden cloud.

"Sure, we'll help," said the angels. "Hang on." So the six Sebastians hung on.

"You need to get airborne," said one angel. "Sure, you do, said the second. "It's no problem," said the angels, "We'll each lend you a wing. We'll only need one each if we join arms and fly together!"

So that is what they did. Each took off one wing. (No, I don't know how they did it.)

Then the angels fixed the wings on to Chuffa's cabin. He carefully flapped one and then the other. Then both at once. And hurrah! He could fly.

Chuffa, the first engine in space! And now for the Moon. Chuffa-chuffa-flap-flap up and up. Sebastian had to give up, it was too high for him. But not for Chuffa.

So the angels guided him to the great, round, dusty surface of the Moon, and on the way, they took turns riding on Chuffa – the very first train ride in space.

Then Chuffa felt himself being pulled like a fish is pulled on a line. But there was no line, just a pull, getting stronger and stronger, and down and down he went until he landed in a moon crater. But it wasn't a hard bump at all. It was as soft and gentle as when you land on your very own bed. No trouble at all. In fact, it was lovely. Chuffa felt as light as a feather.

He began to do kangaroo hops all round the Moon. He even felt like a game of golf or something but he hadn't brought a ball.

"Now, what shall we do next?" asked Chuffa.

"Well, how about a trip to the Great Station-in-the-Sky?" said one of the angels. "That's where all the good trains go, when they get very old. Just give a blast-off on your whistle," said his friends.

That blast-off was enough to launch Chuffa into Outer Space and away beyond that until, they came to a land of beautiful coloured clouds. First a fine blue cloud, where all the engines lived which had come to the end of the line. There, they lived happily ever after without a timetable or anything to worry them. They were very kind to Chuffa and promised that if he were good, one day he could come and live there too!

Then the angels took Chuffa to a rose, pink cloud where even more engines lived. Chuffa was so excited and flapped his wings to keep himself hovering in space. Suddenly, he saw the cutest little engine he had ever seen. She had the prettiest headlights, the sweetest little funnel and the cosiest cabin you ever saw. Which one was it, do you think? Well, we shall never, never know, because at that very moment . . . in spite of the warning voices of the angels, Chuffa decided to land on that rosy, pink cloud and make friends.

"Don't do it," cried the angels. "It won't hold you up. You are too heavy for it." But Chuffa wouldn't listen. WOOOSSH!

Right through that rosy, pink cloud went Chuffa. Down and down and down.

He fell through the pink cloud, past the blue cloud, through Outer Space and down and down.

And as he fell, a terrible thing happened. The speed of his fall loosened the feathers of the wings that could keep him up. One by one, then two by two, they came off and floated away into Outer Space.

Soon there was not a single feather left on either wing and there was nothing to keep him up. Poor old Chuffa was scared. Well, you know how you feel when you dream you are falling downstairs or off the top of a tall tree? That is how Chuffa felt. Down and down you go and nothing can save you.

But just as in a dream, when you fall, you never, never hurt yourself. So it was that Chuffa landed back on his rails without so much as a bump. Not even a teeny one. And there he was, back on Mother Earth with the old Moon shining overhead and old Sebastian fast asleep on his funnel. And there on the cabin roof was a single feather. It MIGHT have been one of Sebastian's feathers. But it might have been an angel's feather. Who can tell? Did Chuffa really go to the Moon, or was it just a dream?

What do you think?

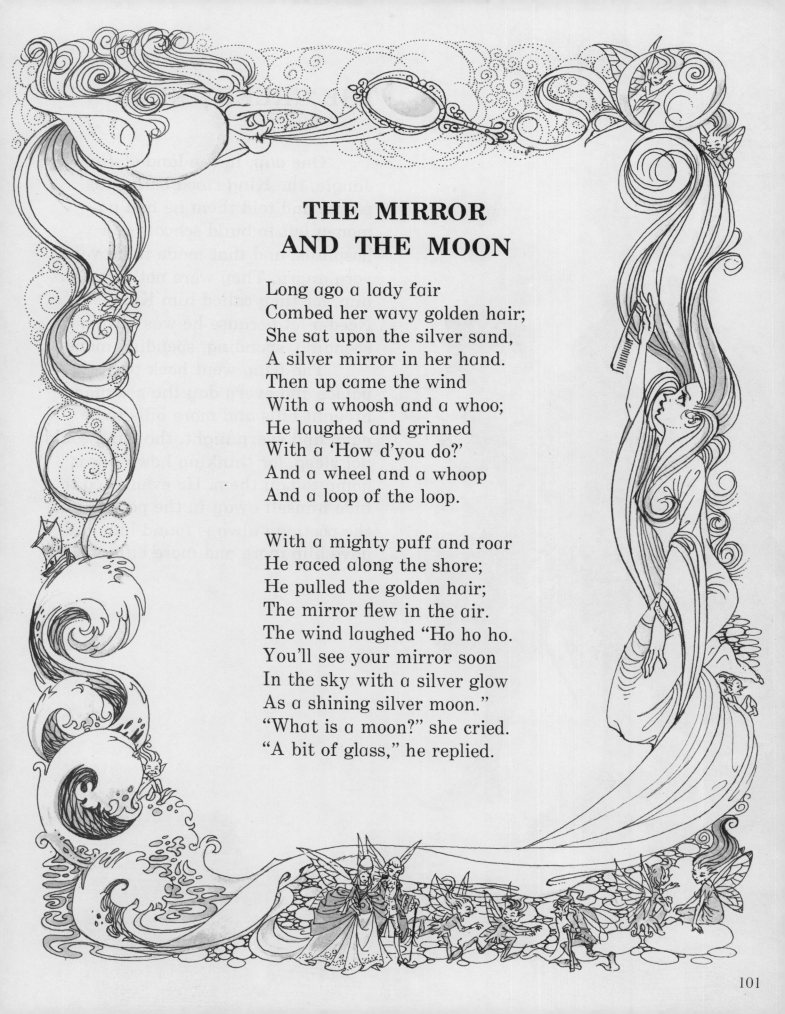

THE MIRROR
AND THE MOON

Long ago a lady fair
Combed her wavy golden hair;
She sat upon the silver sand,
A silver mirror in her hand.
Then up came the wind
With a whoosh and a whoo;
He laughed and grinned
With a 'How d'you do?'
And a wheel and a whoop
And a loop of the loop.

With a mighty puff and roar
He raced along the shore;
He pulled the golden hair;
The mirror flew in the air.
The wind laughed "Ho ho ho.
You'll see your mirror soon
In the sky with a silver glow
As a shining silver moon."
"What is a moon?" she cried.
"A bit of glass," he replied.

THE GREEDY KING

One day, in the land of Jingle Jangle, the King stood before his people and told them he had no money left to build schools and hospitals, and that made them very, very angry. They were not sorry for him, for they called him King Need-a-lot because he was always spending, spending, spending money.

The King went back to his palace and every day the postman brought bills and more bills to be paid, and every night, the King could not sleep, for thinking how he was going to pay them. He even tried to hide himself away in the palace, but the postman always found him and gave him more and more bills.

"I'm getting tired of all these bills," said the King to his old servant. "I think I will run away." And one day he did, and his old servant followed him. As they ran through the town, they passed the Butcher's shop and the Butcher saw them.

"The King is running away and he hasn't paid my bills," he cried. "He must not get away, I'll follow him." So he began to run behind the old servant.

Then they passed the Baker's shop and the Baker saw them.

"The King is running away and he hasn't paid my bills," he cried. "He must not get away, I'll follow him." So he began to run behind the Butcher.

Then they passed the Shoe-maker's shop and the Shoe-maker saw them.

"The King is running away and he hasn't paid my bills," he cried. "He must not get away, I'll follow him." So he began to run behind the Baker.

King Need-a-lot ran on and on and on. He ran over the fields and through the woods until he reached the seashore. He was puffing and blowing and he could not run quickly now. He glanced over his shoulder and saw his old servant, the Butcher, the Baker and the Shoe-maker following him, but as he looked back, he stumbled over a sack on the beach and was just too tired to get up again. When the old servant reached him, he thought the King had hurt himself. He looked round and found a little boat nearby, so he put the King in the boat and ran back to get help.

On the way he met the Butcher, the Baker and the Shoe-maker.

"Stop!" he cried, "The King has hurt himself, we must help him."

He turned round again and ran back to the beach followed by the Butcher, the Baker and the Shoe-maker, but when they reached the seashore, all they could see was the little boat sailing away from the shore and in it was King Need-a-lot fast asleep.

The four of them waited for many, many hours until the tide came in again bringing with it the little boat, and the King was still fast asleep. The Butcher helped the old servant to carry the King back to the woods, while the Baker and the Shoe-maker lifted the sack from the boat and from a hole in one corner dropped a piece of gold and then . . . another and another.

"Why, it's a sack of gold," cried the Baker. "We must carry it carefully and not lose any more."

Away they went to join the others in the woods and there they rested until the King awakened. When he did wake up and saw the Butcher, the Baker and the Shoe-maker sitting beside him, he cried, "I cannot pay you. I've spent all the money and have no more left."

"Oh, yes you have!" they said, and they showed him the sack of gold. "It's yours, you found it."

The King looked puzzled, so his old servant told him all that had happened. He thanked them for taking care of him, then he paid the Butcher's bills, the Baker's bills and the Shoe-maker's bills and they all marched back to town.

The King then paid ALL his bills, gave a big party for everybody who lived in his kingdom and still had enough left to build hospitals and schools for his people.

He never spent all his money ever again and now his people call him King Save-a-lot, because he does.

JUMPING JACK

Jack started jumping
as soon as he could walk;
little jumps at first,
then bigger and bigger.
By the time he had grown
into a young man he found
it easier and quicker to
jump everywhere. People
were rather weary of him.
"There goes 'Jumping
Jack'," they would say.
"It's no good trying
to keep up with him."
His sudden jumps were
startling, and his
neighbours grew to dislike
him. Jack became lonely;
an outsider.

One day, he made up his mind to leave the village where he had lived all his life and go off into the world. He'd walk and walk, for miles and miles; he'd cure himself of jumping. Then, he'd make friends – be an ordinary person. He said goodbye to his parents.

"Don't stay away long, Jack," said his mother. "We shall miss you."

Jack tried to cheer her up. "I'll be back, mother! . . . I'll make my fortune, and get rid of this jumping disease. I don't want to be called 'Jumping Jack' all my life."

His father wished him luck, and they both waved him off on his travels.

After several miles, Jack was tired and quite glad to see a stretch of water in front of him. Leaving his shoes and stockings on the bank, he paddled in the cool waves. Imagine his horror when he saw, swimming towards him, a huge crocodile! . . . What could he do? The creature was so close.

There was only one thing he could do – he jumped!

Landing the other side, on his bare feet, Jack looked around.
There were beautiful flower beds, paths, seats and fountains.

"Good gracious! I've jumped out of one trouble into another!"
he said out loud. "This looks like a royal garden!"

Sure enough, soldiers advanced from all directions, each armed
with a sword. He took another jump – right over their heads! They
gazed up in amazement. Jack looked down towards the courtyard where
he would land; it was straight in front of a splendid palace.

More soldiers rushed, grabbed him and marched him off to the king.
Jack begged His Majesty's pardon for trespassing and explained that
he'd only jumped because he'd been in great danger.

"Quite! Quite!" agreed the king. "You're the first one
Camilla has missed."

Jack gave a shudder at the thought of that terrible crocodile.

Just then, the beautiful Princess Arabella entered and spoke to
her father. He turned to Jack:

"We have other visitors here, competing for my daughter's hand
in marriage. Would you care to join them?"

Jack bowed, first to the princess and then to the king.

"I would be honoured, Your Majesty."

A contest was arranged for that very evening. Jack would have
to fence with a prince, in front of the royal family and hundreds of
people. He had never learned the art of fencing; it would be
difficult and very dangerous.

At first, Jack pranced around keeping himself safe. Then he
gave some jumps. The crowd thought him clever – and funny. People
began to laugh. Soon they were all doubled up with laughter. The
king held his sides. He nearly collapsed when Jack leapt over the
prince's head.

"Stop! Stop!" he cried. "That's enough! . . . I can't laugh
any more!"

Would the king have Jack thrown to Camilla for making the prince look stupid? No; Arabella gave him her hand and they danced round the ball-room. She glanced at his feet.

"They're very nimble, but wouldn't they be more comfortable in shoes?"

Jack felt ashamed, but then he saw her smile.

"Come!" he said and they danced faster and faster. Up the staircase, out of the palace, through the courtyard and garden; on and on they danced to the water's edge. There, Jack lifted Arabella up in his arms and made a flying leap. Camilla's eye gleamed in the light of the moon as she watched them pass over. They landed safely, by the side of Jack's shoes and stockings. He put them on and once more jumped his princess over the water.

Back in the palace, the king made a speech announcing the wedding. Invitations were to be sent to Jack's parents. Jack was to receive a title and the king asked him what name he would like to be called.

"Any name you wish, Your Majesty. I am so happy you could even call me, 'Jumping Jack'!"

DIFFY

Mrs Duck was very happy. She was listening to the little creaks and cracks that meant her eggs were breaking open and soon there would be a family of baby ducklings. One of the eggs kept rolling away and that one did not make any sound at all.

"Now WHY?" Mrs Duck asked herself, staring hard at it.

CREAK! CRACK! POP! went all the other eggs and out popped the fluffy yellow ducklings.

"BEAUTIFUL!" sighed Mrs Duck, happily. She glared at the egg that was left unopened as it rolled away uncracked.

SNAP! Without any warning at all the last egg BURST open and the duckling inside it SHOT out. He went up into the air as if he were a bird who could fly but not swim, instead of a bird that could swim but not fly. Mrs Duck watched open-beaked as the youngest duckling soared into space.

"NOT a budding space-duck!" wailed Mrs Duck, who sometimes watched the Farmer's television.

But the little fellow soon came down to earth again because, of course, he could NOT fly, and he landed upside-down next to his brothers and sisters.

Mrs Duck eyed her son fondly.

"I thought YOU would be different," she said, not knowing whether to be proud or put-out.

"DIFFERENT!" gurgled the little duckling. "What a lovely name. Call me DIFFY!"

The very first thing Diffy wanted to do was to leave home.

"You can't!" snapped Mrs Duck. "You've only just got here."

"I have a SPIRIT OF ADVENTURE," explained Diffy. He had a very good turn of speech, or rather, QUACK, for such a young duckling.

"Save it until you are grown up," shrieked Mrs Duck. She had to shriek because little Diffy was already on his way.

The first place brave Diffy came to was not as adventurous as he thought it might be. HE thought that after all that walking he must have reached foreign parts but he hadn't. He had only got as far as the farmhouse.

The farmer's wife was cleaning the kitchen. She did not like the job and so she was doing it as quickly as she could to get it over. She was rather short-sighted and so when Diffy perched on the handle of a wooden spoon for a rest, she thought he was a feather-duster.

"I had forgotten I had this," she told herself, as she picked up the DIFFYDUCKYWOODENSPOONFEATHERDUSTER.

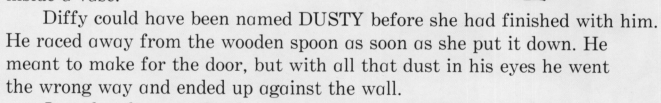

Diffy had to cling hard to that wooden spoon because first the farmer's wife shot him UP to dust the pictures. Then she pushed him SIDEWAYS to dust the clock and even DOWN to dust inside a vase.

Diffy could have been named DUSTY before she had finished with him. He raced away from the wooden spoon as soon as she put it down. He meant to make for the door, but with all that dust in his eyes he went the wrong way and ended up against the wall.

Just then her son, Fred, came in through the door from school. Fred did not see Diffy sitting on the floor trying to brush the dust out of his eyes. Fred took off his hat as soon as he came in, as he always did. He tossed it across the room to try and get it on the hook in the wall above where Diffy was, as he always did. Fred missed, as he always did. The hat fell on the floor as it always did. But never before had there been a baby duckling sitting there, as there was this time. The hat fell over Diffy and at once it did something it had NEVER done before. THE HAT RAN ACROSS THE FLOOR!

It was only Diffy really, who thought the roof had fallen on top of him and was running to try and shake it off.
Fred thought that he was seeing MAGIC and he just stood and watched with eyes like saucers. He closed his eyes so that he could yell louder and at that very moment Diffy reached — and fell over — the doorstep. The hat stayed behind and Diffy was able to scuttle away. When Fred opened his eyes again after his yell, Diffy was gone.

For ever after, Fred was sure that he was the only person in the world who had seen a hat run across a floor. As a matter of fact, he wrote an essay about it at school the next day and got top marks for imagination.

Diffy left his SPIRIT OF ADVENTURE behind him in the farmhouse. He knew that his beak was pointed towards his duckpond home, because he could hear his mother telling his brothers and sisters what to do as she took them for their first swim.

Diffy decided to join them and go back later for his lost SPIRIT OF ADVENTURE. It was sad, in a way, because Mrs Duck could not count and she didn't have time to notice that Diffy was back again. She went on boasting dreadfully to friends and relations about her youngest son, who, she told them, was TRAVELLING THE WORLD WITH A SPIRIT OF ADVENTURE. None of the family and friends could count and so THEY did not know either that Diffy was back, which was a pity for them, because they did get so horribly bored just HEARING about him.

As for Diffy HE never tired of hearing about himself and as he listened hard ALL the time, he grew up feeling that he really was DIFFERENT!

THE BRAVE LITTLE ENGINE

"For goodness' sake, keep still and go to sleep, Bonny!" said the big locomotive.

"I won't get a wink of sleep again tonight if you go on with that fidgeting and shuffling," grumbled a green tanker.

Bonny sighed. He didn't want to keep the other engines in the shed awake. During the day, all he did was to pull a branch line train between a few stations, and he had so much energy left at the end of the day that he simply couldn't go to sleep.

"Bonny's just the engine for the job," said the voice of his driver. The great door of the engine-shed slid open and Joe and the depot manager hurried in.

"It's an emergency," Joe told Bonny. "Two trucks of coal have got to be taken to the power-station tonight. The bridge over the river has been damaged and we daren't risk taking the big goods-engine over it. You are light enough to do it."

Soon Bonny was out of the engine-shed and coupled up to two huge coal-trucks. Never had he had such a load behind him. He puffed and groaned as he felt the weight of the coal-trucks, but he kept pulling, and as he moved forward, the strain eased and he then increased speed. Soon he was rolling along at a smart pace.

"Well done!" said Joe, "I knew you'd do it!"

Bonny had never been out at night before. The moon came out and flooded the track with yellow light. The stars winked down at him and the trees rose like ghosts through the gloom, nodding their branches at him as he rumbled by. Suddenly a great black mouth loomed up in front of him. He let out a screech of fear. He thought he was going to be swallowed up!

"Take it easy!" said Joe. "It's a tunnel, the Cosset Tunnel, half a mile of it."

Bonny had never gone through a tunnel before and the utter darkness of it inside almost sent him into a panic. But he was a plucky little engine, and he gave a blast on his siren, as much as to say, "I'm not afraid of the dark, so here I come!"

Only tiny gleams of light from lamps fixed at long intervals in the sides of the tunnel broke the deep darkness, and presently Bonny became so hot that he thought he would burst his boiler. Then at last he felt a breath of fresh air, and suddenly he came out at the other end of the tunnel.

"Now for the bridge," said Joe. "Be very, very careful.
We don't want to end up in the river!"

Bonny saw two red discs ahead. He knew they were danger
signals. The unsafe bridge stretched right across a wide river.
Joe slowed him down to a crawl, and then Bonny began to roll
across the river. He could see the moonlit water below him on
either side, and he felt the bridge move under the weight of the
trucks behind him.

"Keep going!" muttered Joe, who was very anxious and tense. Very, very slowly, Bonny moved across the bridge, the trucks rumbling behind him. The parapet of the bridge had broken away, but Bonny kept going forward and presently, he heard Joe say, "We're over! Well done, Bonny!"

Bonny let out a whistle of relief, but there was another shock in store for him. Just as if it was attracted by the whistle, a white bird flew suddenly out of a tree beside the track almost right into his funnel! Bonny nearly jumped off the rails!

Joe laughed. "Well, I'm blessed! A snowy owl! It must have thought you were something to eat, Bonny!"

Soon after, they reached the power-station, where the coal-trucks were uncoupled in a siding.

"You've saved all the nearby towns from being blacked out tomorrow," said the power-station manager to Joe. "This coal will keep us going until another load gets here from the north. Thanks for coming!"

Joe patted Bonny. "I've got a first-class engine here," he said. "Now we'd better get back home, Bonny."

Bonny had never been on the main line before. Joe let him have his head – Bonny fairly raced through the night. When he saw the tunnel ahead, he gave a loud shriek and tore into it; he didn't give a hoot for tunnels. He didn't give a hoot for owls, either, even if THEY hooted! But no owls flew his way now. Any birds that were about, took care to keep out of his way as he roared along the line. A herd of cows in a field looked up and called out 'Moo!' to him as he raced past.

"I should think you've broken the speed record tonight, Bonny," said Joe, as he drove him into the engine-shed at the end of his journey. "I shall ask the depot manager if we can have a change from our branch line and pull a train or two on the main line – at least until the bridge is repaired."

In the engine-shed all the engines started to talk at once.

"What happened, Bonny?"

"Where have you been?"

"What was the emergency?"

Bonny gave a great big yawn. "I'll tell you tomorrow," he mumbled. "I'm – too – tired – to – talk – tonight. So – sorry!"

And he fell fast asleep.

THE WEDDING

One day, a little field mouse sat in the middle of a cornfield and waited for her friend Tom. He had a secret to tell, which he whispered in her ear, before they ran off together.

At the edge of the field, grew Red Poppy, now wide awake in the warm September sun. "Good morning," she said to the corn. "You do look well today, quite golden brown in fact."

"I know," said the corn. "And soon I shall be cut down and sent to the miller to be made into flour, but not before the wedding I hope."

"The wedding!" cried Red Poppy looking up at him.

"I use my ears, you know," he said. "Why, only last week I heard Tom Field Mouse telling Milly Field Mouse, that when the moon was full and round in the sky, they would be married the next day, at two o'clock."

"Why, that's today," said Red Poppy, dancing in the breeze.

The little blue harebells, standing on their thin stems said,

"We shall ring for them this afternoon."

The little sparrows, sitting on top of the corn ears said,

"We shall sing for them this afternoon."

"What can we do for them, Red Poppy?" asked the grass growing in the field,

"I'll ask the breeze to help you," she replied.

All week the little field mice had been collecting seeds and berries to eat at the Wedding Day party, and they had asked their cousins from town to come to the wedding and now, all was ready.

The village clock struck two -- Tom and Milly Field Mouse were married. As they walked down the path by Red Poppy, the harebells began to ring, the sparrows began to sing and the breeze blew grass-seed confetti all over them.

Then the party began. There was plenty to eat and then everyone played Hide and Seek, Hunt the Acorn and even had a climbing race to the top of the corn stalks.

"What a lovely wedding we have had," said Milly Field Mouse. "I wonder though, who told our secret."

"Oh, you can't have a secret here, my dear, remember the corn has ears," said Tom and quickly they ran away.

Now, the sun was going down and it was very quiet.

"Goodnight, Red Poppy," said the corn. "I wonder what I shall hear tomorrow?" Red Poppy did not answer, she was fast asleep.

JUMPING FROGS

Once there was a young frog who would not jump. His mother tried to make him jump. His father tried to make him jump. His brothers tried. His sisters tried. But whenever they jumped, or hopped, he walked. And of course, that meant everyone was always having to stop and wait for him, because, as everyone knows, to walk somewhere takes longer than to jump there. His mother was always begging him to hurry. So were his brothers and sisters.

"Jump . . . Francis . . . JUMP!" they would call impatiently, every time they had to stop and wait for him.

"I don't want to jump," Francis would reply.

"Why don't you want to jump?" asked Father Frog one day. He couldn't bear to walk himself, and never did unless it was absolutely necessary.

"Because it's undignified," said Francis.

"Undignified," giggled his brothers and sisters. "You should just see yourself trying to walk."

"Frogs are supposed to jump," said Father Frog. "It's undignified for a frog NOT to jump."

"Perhaps he can't jump," said Mother Frog. She took him along to see the frog doctor. He made Francis lie on the couch and examined his legs carefully.

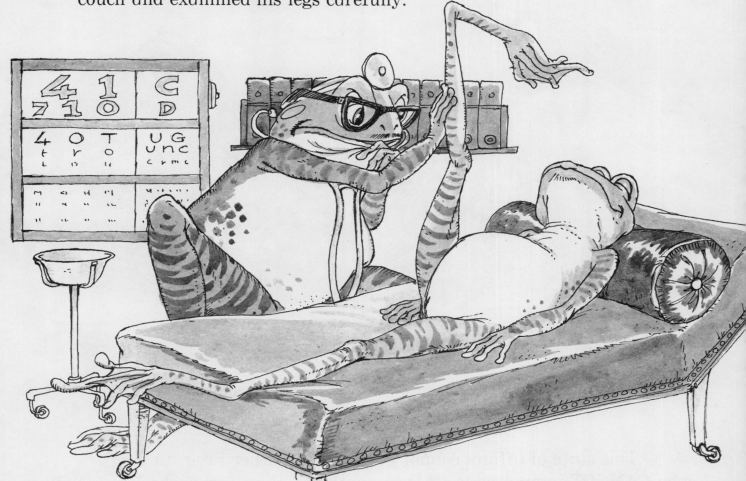

"Stretch . . . bend . . . stretch . . . bend . . ." he said.

Francis did it perfectly. Or rather his legs did. Then the doctor tapped his knees with a rubber hammer to make sure his legs jerked properly. They did. They jerked perfectly.

"Nothing wrong with him at all," said the doctor.

"I knew there wasn't," said Francis.

"Then WHY won't you JUMP?" asked his mother tearfully.

"Because I don't want to," said Francis.

"Because he doesn't want to," said the frog doctor and shook his head wisely. "I'm afraid there's no medicine to cure 'Don't want to's'."

That evening the frog family sent Francis out on an errand and had a family conference.

"This state of affairs cannot go on," said Father Frog. "A frog who CANNOT jump deserves our sympathy . . . but a frog who WILL NOT jump is just being stubborn." Father Frog was getting himself quite worked up. His chins, of which he had several, were beginning to wobble dangerously.

Mother Frog tried to calm him. "Now, now, dear," she said.

"Don't now, now me," grumbled Father Frog. "Just you make that boy jump or I'll never jump again myself . . . and you wouldn't like that would you?"

"Oh no, dear, I wouldn't," said Mother Frog, and then she added thoughtfully, "But I wonder . . ."

"Wonder what?" interrupted Father Frog crossly.

"I wonder what would happen if we ALL walked everywhere . . ." said Mother Frog quickly because Father Frog's fourth chin was beginning to wobble now.

"We would look silly – everyone would laugh at us," said Father Frog. "And I would lose my temper . . . in fact, I think I'm going to lose it anyway . . ."

"Now, now, dear," said Mother Frog soothingly. THAT did it, of course. Father Frog jumped up and down, stamping both feet at once, till HE ran out of breath and his legs ran out of spring.

"Feel better dear?" asked Mother Frog when at last he stopped. She had washed the supper dishes and the children had gone to bed.

"Yes . . ." said Father Frog. ". . . and I've been thinking. Make US look ridiculous would he? Well, we'll make HIM look ridiculous then perhaps he'll change his mind about walking everywhere.

"Now, now, dear," said Mother Frog, but that time, fortunately, Father Frog didn't appear to hear, or perhaps, if he did, he was just too tired to lose his temper again.

Father Frog told the family that they too, must walk everywhere. They found it a very difficult thing to do, for it is as natural for a frog to jump as it is for a tree to grow. They had to concentrate really hard and went about with deep frowns on their faces. Francis was quick to notice that no one was smiling, and that worried him, but then he noticed they weren't jumping either, and THAT pleased him.

"You're being sensible at last," he said happily. "Now I have a family I can be proud of."

Father Frog spluttered and got very red.

"It's not going to work . . ." he muttered under his breath. "If it doesn't . . . I'll . . . I'll . . ."

But in spite of Father Frog's doubts, the whole family tried. How hard it was, pretending not to hear the scornful laughter of the other frogs. How tired their legs got. How short their tempers became. Francis was used to walking. HIS legs never got tired, and although it still took him a long time to walk everywhere, he always got there much quicker than the rest of the family. Now it was HIS turn to stand and wait while everyone caught up with HIM.

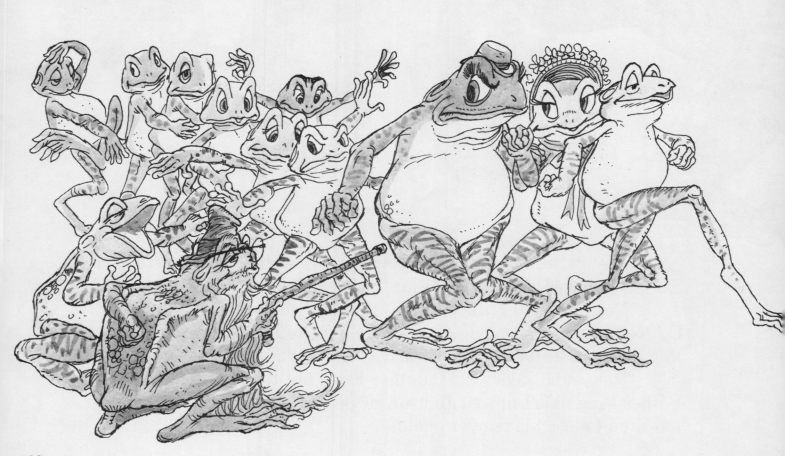

"Oh do hurry up!" he said one morning, when there had been a shower of rain and everyone was on his way to the puddle patch. "The sun will dry up the puddles before we get there."

Father Frog signalled secretly to the rest of the family to slow down even more.

The sun was warm. Francis could feel it drying his back. He wanted to get into some nice, cool, wet, water.

"We'll all dry up, and frizzle away!" he grumbled. "If you can't walk any faster than that, why don't you jump?"

"What was that you said?" asked Father Frog, pretending he hadn't heard properly.

"Jump . . . JUMP!" shouted Francis, losing HIS temper, because he was dry and hot, and everyone else was being silly. "Look, like this . . . I'll show you . . . jump . . . JUMP . . ."

And there he was, jumping like a proper frog should.

"Thank goodness for that," sighed his mother and father.

"Hurrah!" shouted his brothers and sisters, and raced him to the puddle patch.

From that day onwards Francis jumped everywhere, as a frog should, and to his surprise he found he enjoyed it. He even won prizes for jumping, and THAT, as Father Frog said, is as dignified as a frog can get.

CHUFFA AND THE BANDIT

Way up in the North there is a great big fir forest, and in the forest there are many wild creatures like birds and bees, and butterflies and rabbits, and badgers and beavers and bears. There is also a railway line for carrying logs from the fir forest. And on this line goes Chuffa the train, driven by old Mr Driver. He is always ready to give anyone a lift and all the animals love him. And Chuffa too! Chuff chuff chuffa-chuffa-chuffa.

Now, one day some little birds flew up and said, "Oh, Mr Driver, do come and have a look at Bruin the Bear. He is very poorly."

Mr Driver jammed on the brakes. ('I wish he wouldn't do that,' thought Chuffa.) Old Mr Driver got down from the train and the birds led him into the forest. There was Bruin the Bear propped up against a fir tree looking, very, very poorly.

"Why, what's up Bruin?" asked Mr Driver.

But Bruin could only sigh. "Just hand me your paw," said old Mr Driver, and he took out his watch and felt Bruin's pulse.

"My, my, that's very fast, or else my watch is slow. You certainly are a poorly bear. We shall have to get you to old Doc. Sawbones. He'll fix you up in a jiffy."

Well, it wasn't all that easy getting Bruin on the train. He was weak and limp and floppy and they had to pull him and push him and lift him.

"Gee, I feel poorly," said Bruin.

"Never you mind, old fellow," said old Mr Driver. "Just a few more steps and you'll soon be on the train and on your way to the Doctor." At last they managed to shove him and push him and pull him into an empty truck.

"Ready?" said Mr Driver to Chuffa.

"Wooo-oo-oo," replied Chuffa and off they went. Chuffa-chuff-achuff-achuff-achuffa.

And of course they were late! The Station Master at Dallas was as cross as can be. "Just look at the time," he shouted. "Half an hour late! Half an hour!"

"I'm sorry. I couldn't help it," said Mr Driver. "I found a poorly bear." And he showed the Station Master poor old Bruin. But that didn't please the Station Master either.

"Get that darned bear out of here," he yelled.

"I cannot," said Mr Driver. "He cannot walk and I cannot lift him. He is too poorly to walk."

"Then put him on a trolley. Do anything but get him out of here. Do you hear?"

"Yes," said old Mr Driver.

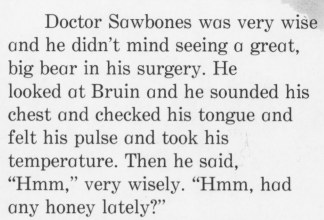

Doctor Sawbones was very wise and he didn't mind seeing a great, big bear in his surgery. He looked at Bruin and he sounded his chest and checked his tongue and felt his pulse and took his temperature. Then he said, "Hmm," very wisely. "Hmm, had any honey lately?"

The bear groaned. "Honey?" he said weakly. "Did you say honey? Well, perhaps just a taste."

"How much?" asked the Doctor.

"Well, w-e-l-l, about two pounds, maybe three," said the poor, sick bear.

"Right, into bed for three days. That'll put you right. And no more honey for a month."

And just as the Doctor said, in a few days the bear was quite well again and fit enough to go back to the forest. So old Mr Driver fetched Chuffa along and they set off for the fir forest. Chuff chuff chuffa chuffa-chuffa . . .

When they got there, the bear climbed down and said to kind-hearted Mr Driver, "Thank you very much for helping me when I was poorly. If ever you are in this forest and want any help, just call out 'Bruin' and I'll be there at once."

"Well, that is very kind of you," said Mr Driver. "I do hope I shall not need to call for help."

"So do I," said Bruin, "but you never can tell."

Back at the railway station, the Sheriff had a job for Mr Driver and Chuffa.

"Just listen to the Sheriff," said the Station Master. (But someone else was listening to the Sheriff. Who could it be?)

"I want you to take this bag of money to Woodville, see?" said
the Sheriff. (But someone else saw as well. Who could it be?)

"See no one steals it. Understand?" (But someone else understood
as well! Who could it be?) Mr Driver said he would take the money
for the Sheriff.

He took the money in the bag and hid it under some logs in the
train. Then he pulled the lever and off they went. C-h-u-f-f
chuff chuffa chuffa-chuffa . . .

All was going well as they went whisking through the forest, when
suddenly Chuffa saw a great pile of logs ahead right on the railway
line. He whistled like anything and Mr Driver jammed on the brakes.
('I wish he wouldn't do that,' thought Chuffa.)

Mr Driver got down and looked at the logs. "Something strange
going on down here," he said wisely. Then he began to shift the
logs from the line. Suddenly he heard a most terrible shout.

"STICK 'EM UP!" roared a voice.

And there beside the track was a bold, bad Bandit. With a bandit's horse. And a bandit's mask. And a bandit's gun! Poor Mr Driver had to put his hands up in the air.

"Now, where's that money?" shouted the Bandit.

"In the wood," said Mr Driver.

"And where's the wood?" cried the Bandit.

"Under the trees," said Mr Driver truthfully.

"Then I'll give you three seconds to find it," said that horrid Bandit, "Then, I'll fire."

So what could Mr Driver do but get the bag from under the wood.

"If you steal it, it won't do you any good you know," he said to the Bandit. "If you're a thief, you'll always find there's trouble brewing."

And as he said that, up popped Bruin the Bear! Like a flash he seized the bad Bandit's hat and pulled it down over his eyes.

At the sight of the bear, the bad Bandit's horse bolted, and the Bandit's gun went off BANG! But Bruin held on tight until Mr Driver brought a rope. Then they tied him up so that he could not escape and set him on top of some logs in one of the trucks.

"Come on Chuffa, my lad," said old Mr Driver. "Off we go to Woodville as quick as quick." Bruin said, "I think I'll get on as well, to keep an eye on this gentleman here." (He meant the Bandit.) So he got up on the next truck and kept a sharp eye on the Bandit who was too scared to move.

"Just as well you remembered to call out 'Bruin' like I said," said the bear.

"Wasn't it!" said Mr Driver who didn't know what he was talking about.

"Do you suppose there is a reward for this bandit?" Chuffa said. "Woo-oo-oo woo-oo-oo chuffa chuffa . . ."

When they reached Woodville, Mr Driver handed the money over to the Bank Manager. "Capital, capital," cried the Bank Manager. Then Mr Driver handed the Bandit over to the Sheriff. "Splendid, splendid," cried the Sheriff. Everyone in Woodville was delighted and there WAS a reward for the bold, bad Bandit. And the next day, Mr Driver and Bruin were given Sheriff's Deputy badges.

"I owe it all to Bruin," said Mr Driver.

"And I owe it all to Chuffa," said Bruin.

"And so do I," said Mr Driver, proudly patting Chuffa.

"Well done, Chuffa. Well done indeed."

COME TO THE FAIR

I'll see you at the fair.
It's great fun to be there,
With merry shouts
From the roundabouts,
And the big wheel in the air.

It isn't very far;
We'll drive a dodgem car,
With a bang and a smash
And a prang and a crash,
And win a goldfish in a jar.

We'll have a good try
At the coconut shy;
We'll throw with a ring,
We'll ride on a swing
And make it go up to the sky.

I'll see you at the fair.
It's great fun to be there,
With merry shouts
From the roundabouts,
And the big wheel in the air.

THE NEW COAT

Pimm Pixie was rolling up cobweb thread in the brambles one day, when his coat caught on a thorn, and tore from the collar right down to the hem. It was as open down the back as it was down the front.

"I suppose I could put some buttons on it," he said, "but then everyone would think I had my head on back to front."

When he got home he mended the tear but he knew the coat would never be the same.

"I can't see the mend myself," he said, "but everyone else can. Everyone will be looking at my stitches, which I know are very uneven. I think it's time I had a new coat."

He went to see the pixie tailor.

"Good morning Pimm," said the tailor. "What can I do for you?"

"I want a new coat, exactly like this one," said Pimm. The torn coat had a deep collar to turn up round his ears when the wind blew, it was long enough to keep his knees warm, and it had deep pockets for carrying things in. He felt comfortable in it. He liked wearing it and saw no reason why his new coat should be any different.

"I'll be glad to make it for you," said the tailor, who had made Pimm's first coat and was glad he liked it so much. He took Pimm's measurements, just to make sure they were still the same, which they were, pixies not being in the habit of growing very much

"There is one small change I would like you to make," said Pimm, who had been looking at the tailor's own coat.

"Yes?" said the tailor, waiting with his pencil held over his note pad.

"I would like it made up in a different shade of green this time . . . I like the shade you are wearing."

The tailor wrote, 'colour, emerald green' on his note pad.

"When will it be ready?" asked Pimm. His own sewing was not very good. The draughts were finding their way in, in between his clumsy stitches and his back was getting cold.

"Tomorrow, if I start straight away," said the tailor, and he went to the shelf and took down a roll of emerald green cloth.

"Ummmm" said Pimm thoughtfully, as the tailor started to snip with his scissors. Pixie tailors can start cutting straight away, they don't have to bother with paper patterns. "Perhaps that blue would be better."

"But I've already started cutting," said the tailor.

"It's my coat. I'm the one who will have to wear it. The colour MUST be right."

The tailor put down his scissors. "If you want your coat finished by tomorrow," he said, "you must make up your mind quickly. I will give you until eleven o'clock."

"I'll go away, and think about it, and then come back and tell you what I have decided," said Pimm. Before he reached the door he turned and said, "I've thought already. Make it in crimson."

"Very well . . . if you're QUITE sure," said the tailor.

Pimm said he WAS sure, but five minutes later he was back.

"I've changed my mind. I'll have it made in yellow."

Ten minutes later he had decided on indigo. And ten minutes after that, he had decided on purple.

"I do wish you'd make up your mind," sighed the tailor.

"I am making up my mind," said Pimm. "I've made it up six times already."

The tailor put ALL the rolls of cloth on the table.

"Now which is it to be?" he said, beginning to look almost as sharp and scratchy as his pins. "I can't have you changing your mind any more. I have other customers to think about."

"The trouble is," wailed Pimm, "I like ALL the colours. It really is very difficult to choose just one."

"Then leave the choice to me," said the tailor. It seemed to Pimm that perhaps that might be the best idea.

"Come back in the morning," said the tailor. "If I see your nose peeping round that door before morning, I'll snip it off with my scissors." He didn't mean that, of course, but he had to keep Pimm out of his way somehow. "Now be off with you!"

Pimm hardly slept a wink all night wondering what colour cloth the tailor would use.

Next morning, as soon as it was light, he went and stood on the tailor's doorstep. It was hours before the tailor opened the door. He knew Pimm was there, but he had his breakfast first, swept the floor and tidied the shelves. He didn't think it would do Pimm any harm to keep him waiting. At nine o'clock precisely, by the dandelion clock, he unbolted the door and let Pimm in.

"Is it finished? What colour did you use? Let me see it. Oh, I do hope you used the RIGHT colour!"

"Which colour IS the right colour?" asked the tailor.

"I don't know . . . if only I DID know . . . " wailed Pimm.

He could hardly bear to look as the tailor uncovered the coat. What could he say if he didn't like the colour the tailor had chosen? But what a surprise he had. He gasped! He clapped his hands together in glee! He jumped onto the table and danced a jig! He beamed from ear to ear! The point on his hat curled and uncurled by itself! The tailor looked pleased.

"Did I use the right colour?" he asked, dodging out of the way as Pimm bounced up and down like a ball.

"Oh you did! You did!" exclaimed Pimm. "What a clever tailor you are!"

The tailor blushed with pleasure.

"Try it on for size," he said. It fitted perfectly, as he knew it would because he had taken the measurements himself.

"Thank you . . . thank you . . . thank you . . ." sang Pimm as he danced off down the street. The clever tailor had used a piece of cloth from each roll and had made him a coat that was ALL the colours of the rainbow!

SOLDIERS

Ten wooden pegs,
Smooth and brown,
On the table,
Lying down.

Black for boots,
And black for hats,
Red for tunics,
Front and back.
Dark blue legs,
With stripes of white.
Spots of gold,
For buttons bright.

Ten soldiers made
From wooden pegs,
March up and down
On painted legs.

THE BELLS

It was a warm night. The stars were twinkling and the moon kept popping in and out of the clouds.

"Ho de hi o hum hum hum!" sang Bartholomew Green at the very top of his voice as he ambled along the lane past the churchyard.

"Hoohoo!" hooted an owl from within a hollow tree.

"Hoo hoo to yooo tooo!" sang out Bartholomew Green. He had been to a party which he had enjoyed very much and now he was on his way home. He didn't care that everyone else was in bed and asleep. He wanted everyone to be as happy as he was.

"Hi de ho hum hum hum!" he sang as he stumbled along the dark path by the vicarage gate.

Inside the vicarage, the vicar put his head under the bedclothes and pretended he couldn't hear the noise going on beneath his bedroom window. He knew who the reveller was . . . it was Bartholomew Green. He would have recognized that voice anywhere. He wished Bartholomew Green would go to bed at the same time as everyone else.

144

But the vicar couldn't possibly pretend the noise wasn't there. There was a rattle at the window.

Bartholomew Green was throwing gravel.

There was a much heavier rattle against the window. Bartholomew Green was throwing tiny stones. If he wasn't careful he would break the glass.

The vicar opened the window wearily, and leant out.

"Go away . . ." he said. "Please . . . go away."

"Ring the bells," called Bartholomew Green. "Ring the bells . . . I want to hear the bells . . ."

"No," said the vicar. "I will not ring the bells." And he closed his bedroom window with such a bang that Bartholomew Green knew he meant what he said.

Now, it so happened that Bartholomew wasn't the only person out that night. There was a wizard slinking around dark, night-time corners and dipping into dark, night-time pools, looking for spell-making ingredients. He came upon Bartholomew Green sitting on a tombstone, crying slow silent tears that rolled like raindrops down the side of his nose.

"What's wrong?" asked the wizard, who had found all that he had wanted to find and was in a good mood.

"He won't ring the bells!" said Bartholomew Green. "I asked, but Vicar won't ring the bells . . ."

145

"Then I will ring them for you," said the wizard, who felt like playing a joke on someone. He fumbled in his pocket and took out some red powder mixed with pocket fluff, and flicked it towards the vicar's bedroom window.

"There." he said. "That should do it."

"I can't hear anything," said Bartholomew Green. He could see something though. The light had gone on in the vicar's bedroom and the vicar was dancing about with his hands over his ears.

The wizard laughed. "He should have done as you asked," he said.

The next day there were rumours all over the village.

"Have you heard? The vicarage is haunted. Bells have been ringing."

"I haven't heard anything," said Bartholomew Green.

"You wouldn't . . . they're only heard in the bedroom. Maisie told us about it . . . she dusts and cleans for the vicar you know. The vicar didn't have a wink of sleep last night."

Bartholomew had some hazy memory of asking the vicar to ring the bells the night before, and he also had a hazy memory of meeting a friendly person in a long robe in the churchyard . . . but he couldn't remember anything else. So he went to the vicarage to hear for himself.

The rumours were perfectly true. Outside the vicarage it was so quiet he could hear the grasshoppers chirping. Inside the house it was so quiet he could hear the bread singing in the oven. But in the vicar's bedroom, which by then was crowded with people who had come to hear for themselves, there was a merry jangle of noise.

Clang! Clang! Clang! Clang! Clang!

Bartholomew couldn't help feeling that somehow it was his fault, though he couldn't for the life of him think why.

The bells continued to ring in the vicar's bedroom for years and years. He got quite used to them in the end and could sleep in spite of the noise. Then one night, on the same night that the wizard died, as it happened, though nobody noticed the coincidence, they stopped ringing as mysteriously as they had begun. The vicar almost missed their cheerful company. As for Bartholomew, he never quite lost that strange guilty feeling he had. It was something he often found himself wondering about, even when he was an old, old man.

AMANDA AND THE ANIMALS

Once upon a time, there was a little girl called Amanda, who lived in a pretty white house in the country with her mother and father.

One sunny day, as it was her birthday, and so, of course, a very special day, they took her to the zoo. Amanda was so excited, for it was the first time she had ever been there and she adored animals.

She gazed in wonder at the huge lions, laughed at the antics of the cheeky monkeys, and stroked the heads of the gentle deer. She had a wonderful time!

Later that day, tired but happy, she sat on her garden swing while her mother prepared supper -- a special birthday supper -- with a birthday cake as well.

Amanda swung slowly backwards and forwards, her mind full of all the animals she'd seen at the zoo, some so big; some so small; and all the time she swung, backwards and forwards, backwards and forwards . . .

'In the jungle, I'm a king,'
Remarked the Lion full of pride,
'I'm not afraid of anything,
At least, not much,' he said aside.

'I know the big savannah well,
There, many animals retreat.
But I must find out where they dwell,
For when I'm hungry, I must eat.'

Amanda's blue eyes widened as she looked at the lion. He
certainly was beautiful, with his thick golden mane and his
flashing eyes. As a matter of fact, he was sitting on her
father's prize roses, but she didn't like to tell him, in case
he was offended. He went on . . .

'My claws are very sharp, you know,
Because they have to grasp and tear.
My sense of smell is not so good,
But there's very little I don't hear.

At night, I see as well as day,
And I can run quite fast along,
Though rarely do I chase my prey,
For I am very, very strong.'

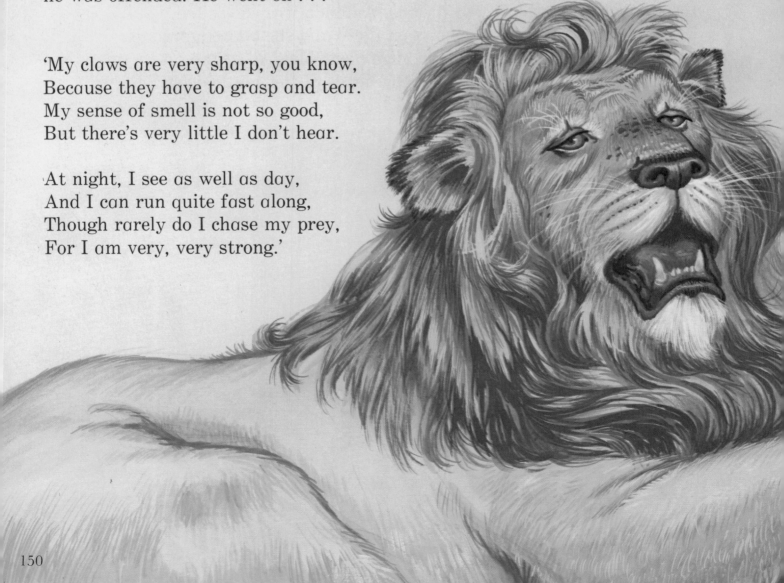

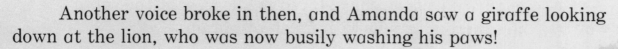

Another voice broke in then, and Amanda saw a giraffe looking down at the lion, who was now busily washing his paws!

'What of me?' asked the Giraffe,
I'm very tall, quite eighteen feet.
My neck is long,' he gave a laugh,
'So from the tall trees I can eat.

My eyes are fringed against the sun.
I've two horns on my head.
I have no voice at all -- just none,
I cannot even howl instead!

I live in Africa -- it's hot,
The sun is always big and bright,
It seems to shine an awful lot,
The only time it's cool is night.

It's quite a problem when I drink,
I have to put my legs astride,
Yet though I'm tall, I really think
I'm quite content and satisfied.'

Amanda chuckled at this, then stared in surprise at the zebra
who was standing there listening with much attention.

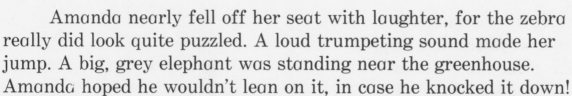

'My stripes blend in with the trees,
And with the background where I live.
I come and go just as I please,
Though lots of care to this I give!'

On one point I should like some light
About these stripes upon my back.
Now what is which, I don't know quite—
Black stripe on white or white on black?'

Amanda nearly fell off her seat with laughter, for the zebra
really did look quite puzzled. A loud trumpeting sound made her
jump. A big, grey elephant was standing near the greenhouse.
Amanda hoped he wouldn't lean on it, in case he knocked it down!

'In size I'm larger than you all,
For quite six tons -- that's what I weigh.
I trumpet loudly when I call,
So they can hear me far away.

You'd think my trunk was in the way,
And yet without it lost I'd be,
For when I'm hungry through the day,
I pick leaves from the highest tree.

Some of my friends, they work for man,
They pull and lift the trunks of trees,
That's not for me, for if I can
I'd rather do just what I please.'

The elephant thought hard for a moment, swinging his trunk from side to side, until Amanda knew she'd simply burst if she didn't laugh soon, but she didn't dare!

The elephant continued,

'My ears are big; my hide is grey,
I have two tusks of ivory;
I've nothing really more to say,
Except I'm rather glad I'm me!'

Here he was interrupted by a sniffly, snuffly sort of voice.

'I know I am an ugly beast,
But all Hippos are just like me;
And I don't mind it in the least,
There's nothing else I'd rather be!

You'd see that just my head appears
When I am swimming, which I love;
For I also close my nose and ears,
That's all you notice from above.'

The hippopotamus stopped short then, his words almost drowned when he opened his enormous mouth to have a big, comfortable yawn! Amanda couldn't believe her eyes. How could any animal have such a huge mouth?

'I'm twelve feet long, that's quite a lot,
I weigh four tons, or so it's said.
My feet are webbed, so I can trot
Along the muddy river-bed.

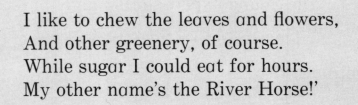

I like to chew the leaves and flowers,
And other greenery, of course.
While sugar I could eat for hours.
My other name's the River Horse!'

Amanda was surprised to hear this, and thought it was a lovely name. The Hippo looked at her, his little eyes twinkling, gave another yawn, and promptly went to sleep!

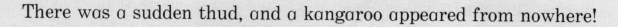

There was a sudden thud, and a kangaroo appeared from nowhere!

'I know I'm not as big as you,
Nor quite as heavy, nor as plump;
But there's one thing that you can't do,
That I can do, and that is JUMP!

I leap as far as twenty feet,
The farmers wish I could be banned,
Because you see, I love to eat
The grass that grows upon their land.

When I was born, you'd never dream
That I was very, very small,
So very tiny, it would seem
I wasn't really there at all!

Within my mother's pouch I kept,
Though that's a long time past, I own.
Inside it, nice and warm I slept,
But now I'm big and fully-grown.'

Even as he finished, all the other animals who had been listening, started to make such a noise, each one claiming that he was the finest animal. Amanda put her hands on her ears to shut out the noise, but it grew louder and louder, until suddenly she heard above it all, someone calling her name.

"Amanda, supper's ready!" It was her mother calling. She turned to look at the animals again, but they all seemed to have disappeared somewhere.

"What a shame," she said, "I was so enjoying myself!" She raced down the garden path and went into the house.

"Mummy, I've just seen some of the animals that we saw at the zoo today!" Amanda told her excitedly.

Her mother smiled down at her. "Oh, Amanda," she laughed, "have you been playing make-believe again?" Amanda opened her mouth to argue, but shut it again. She knew it wasn't any good anyway, because whenever she'd had an adventure before, and told her mother, she'd always said Amanda had been playing make-believe. Grown-ups didn't know everything, did they?